"I offer myself as a fill-in for Dave."

"A fill-in?" Brooke echoed blankly.

"I'll put it plainly, Brooke. Dave's a good friend of mine and so is his wife. With a little luck and no distractions—" Kley looked at her pointedly "—they might be able to salvage what began as a good marriage. So perhaps I could persuade you to leave them to sort themselves out. I've no commitments, and I'm sure you and I could have some interesting times...."

The sound of her hand contacting his cheek echoed around them.

"I'm sorry. I shouldn't have done that," she said. "But you must admit I was provoked."

"At least we know where we stand," Kley said at last. "But my warning still goes. Keep away from Dave."

"I'm not..." Brooke gave in. "Oh, what's the use!"

Books by Lynsey Stevens

HARLEQUIN ROMANCE

HARLEQUIN PRESENTS

These books may be available at your local bookseller.

Don't miss any of our special offers. Write to us at the following address for information on our newest releases.

Harlequin Reader Service
P.O. Box 52040, Phoenix, AZ 85072-2040
Canadian address: P.O. Box 2800, Postal Station A,
5170 Yonge St., Willowdale, Ont. M2N 6J3

Terebori's Gold

Lynsey Stevens

Harlequin Books

TORONTO • NEW YORK • LONDON
AMSTERDAM • PARIS • SYDNEY • HAMBURG
STOCKHOLM • ATHENS • TOKYO • MILAN

Original hardcover edition published in 1981
by Mills & Boon Limited

ISBN 0-373-02706-0

Harlequin Romance first edition July 1985

CHAPTER ONE

THE usual cacophony of children's voices reverberated about the six blocks of classrooms, but Brooke Drynan was so used to the sound that it barely penetrated her consciousness. She was inside herself, existing in her cocoon of indifference, a protectiveness that she had woven around herself over the past year. Her thick fair hair was pulled halfheartedly back into a prim bob at her nape and heavy glasses sat firmly on her nose.

Perhaps it was her flat rubber-soled shoes or the louder than average volume of little voices that made her approach to the staffroom pass unnoticed by the three teachers already in occupation, but the sound of her name being spoken caused Brooke's footsteps to falter before she reached the doorway.

'You're supposed to be Brooke's friend, Kath, her best friend, and we can't understand why you haven't said something,' the physical education teacher, Jilly Martin, was saying.

'What exactly would you have me say, Jilly? Look, Brooke, I'm your best friend, so I think I should tell you that just because a girl gets jilted it doesn't mean she has to let herself turn into a frump. Come off it, Jilly, I'm not as hardhearted as you are,' exclaimed Kath Barton, who had grown up with Brooke and had always been a special friend.

Brooke blinked, not even feeling shock as the meaning of those words filtered through her mind, a mind which seemed to be turning with painful slowness. She had schooled her thoughts and expressions too well over the past months for her to show any outward sign that the unmalicious barbs had found their mark.

'Sometimes you have to be cruel to be kind,' stated

Barbara Jones, a commercial teacher.

'Well, someone else can be kind to Brooke. I just couldn't bring myself to do it,' said Kath. 'For all the brave front and stiff upper lip, I think she's still pretty vulnerable about the whole thing. Honestly,' she ejaculated, 'even now I could cheerfully throttle that . . . that lily-livered, weak-kneed Stephen Marsh, except that I think Brooke's well rid of him. I always did feel she was far too good for him.'

'Yes, I agree with you there,' said Jilly. 'I only met him a couple of times and I wasn't impressed. But that still leaves our problem unsolved. What are we going to do about Brooke? It goes against my grain for her to be allowed to settle more firmly each day into that shallow little rut of hers. It's a downright waste! She used to be so attractive, so vivacious. If we hadn't known her at college I'd say the Brooke Drynan of a couple of years ago was a totally different girl. Heavens, Kath, it's a positive sin! I wish I had her figure and that gorgeous hair,' said Jilly, who was dark and petite, for all her exertions involved with teaching physical education.

'And what happened to all the great gear she had?' asked Barbara. 'Now it's always plain old skirts and blouses and flat, sensible shoes. Something will have to be done. We can't sit back without making some effort to shock her out of it and bring her back to the present.'

There was a moment's silence while Brooke remained poised on the verandah, unable to move. Only this scene existed in that moment in time and even the shrill voices of the students had faded into the background.

'What say I arrange a blind date for her? A friend of mine—remember Greg?—has a couple of nice single fellows working with him,' suggested Jilly. 'Do you think Brooke would agree to come out for dinner or a show one night if I set it up with Greg?'

'I don't think she would, not at the moment anyway,' replied Kath unhappily. 'I'm not sure that's the answer,

Jilly. Stephen Marsh was the first fellow she was ever seriously interested in, so I don't think we should rush into matchmaking. I'd just like to see her snap out of the cool, unapproachable, "keep your distance" little world she exists in these days.'

'Well, I for one wouldn't say no to a blind date with a nice single man, Jilly,' said Barbara as the bell sounded.

Brooke forced herself to move, taking a couple of steps backwards so that it appeared she was in the act of walking up to the staffroom as the three girls hurried out, heading for their various classes.

'Oh, hi, Brooke,' Kath greeted her friend, her face a little pink. 'You're back late from lunch.'

Brooke forced a smile. 'Yes, I had to slip down to the shops to collect some material my mother ordered and I took longer than I expected. I've got a free period now so, no matter, I'll have a bite of lunch while I'm marking papers.'

Both Jilly and Barbara had gone on ahead.

'Well, I'll see you after work, then,' said Kath, following the other two along the corridor.

It wasn't until she had finally crept into bed that night that Brooke allowed herself to think about what she had inadvertently overheard. She had determinedly kept her mind on her classes during the afternoon and now, as she tried to push the scene from her mind, each time she closed her eyes she heard Kath's voice. 'She's turned into a frump!' Brooke tossed restlessly. A frump. How could Kath say that? She was supposed to be her friend. Was she a frump? Was that how everyone saw her?

She climbed out of bed and flicked on the light over her dressing table. Peering shortsightedly at her reflection, she picked up her glasses and shoved them on her nose, gazing critically at the face looking back at her. Her hair, unrestrained by its usual band, fell a little listlessly to halfway down her back, the weight of it curtailing somewhat its tendency to spring into natural waves. The lamplight deepened its pure golden colour, darker now as she had not spent much time outdoors lately in the bleaching glow of the sun. It had grown in the past year, longer than she had ever worn it. She just hadn't bothered to have it cut back to her usual shoulder length. There didn't seem to be any point.

Her eyes were her best feature, she felt, large and blue and fringed by long brown lashes, not really needing more than a touch of mascara. How long was it since she had applied any make-up? Taken the trouble to add more than a touch of lipstick? She hadn't bothered with eye make-up when she wore her glasses.

And what about your contact lenses? she asked herself. Once again it was all too much bother, too much of an effort when she could just slip on her glasses. She had always worn them before.... She stopped. Go on, she goaded herself, say it. You always wore your contact lenses, and make-up, and pretty, attractive clothes before ... before Stephen left you. There, you admitted it. Before Stephen left you, deciding he loved someone else more than he loved you.

Brooke stood up and paced across the carpet in her bare feet. It was almost a year since they were to have been married. The year had passed so quickly it seemed like just yesterday. One minute she had been gliding along on a cloud of happiness and the next her world had shattered about her.

She had met Stephen Marsh at teachers' training college. They had been kindred spirits, on the same wavelength, drawn to each other right from the first, and spent all their spare time in each other's company. They were an accepted pair and Stephen had become one of the Drynan family. He was an only child brought up by an elderly aunt and he had often told Brooke how marvellous he thought it was of her parents to make him so welcome in the midst of their family. They had all liked Stephen. He had charm.

Brooke tried to recall his face to mind and, with a shock, realised she could only bring a hazy image into focus. She opened the bottom drawer of her dressing table and lifted a framed photograph from beneath a pile of discarded clothing. Stephen Marsh's face smiled back. It was a very good likeness of the handsome young man. And he was handsome. Tall, fair, sun-tanned, with a ready smile and the knack of saying the right things at the right time with genuine sincerity, or so she had thought.

Since their first meeting Brooke had been interested in no one but Stephen. Her world had revolved around him and she was sure he had felt the same way about her; she would have staked her life on it. Until her cousin had arrived from Sydney two weeks before the wedding. Samantha, Brooke's mother's sister's only child, was four years younger than Brooke and the exact opposite in looks and temperament. Samantha was short, with light brown hair and huge brown eyes and a helpless aura that drew masculine protectiveness like a magnet.

Stephen and Brooke had never had a disagreement until two days before Samantha's arrival, when Brooke had found herself alone in the house with Stephen for the first time in ages and they had had what had amounted to their first and last quarrel. Wedding arrangements, dress fittings, etc., had kept Brooke busy, and to sit with Stephen on the covered patio of her parents' home had been pure bliss. They had relaxed, side by side, on the swinging patio chair bathed in moonlight. Stephen had kissed her passionately, a little more fiercely than he had before and, because she had missed him and wanted to reassure him of her love, Brooke had returned his kisses a little more freely than she usually did.

From there things had got out of hand, ending with Brooke having to push him away, again something she had never had to do with Stephen previously. He had been angry and accused her of being a prude, not understanding her need to wait until they were married before they became physically one. They would be man and wife in two weeks anyway, he said. After some time and much discussion they had made friends again and Stephen had apologised grudgingly for his behaviour, although the whole thing had left Brooke feeling hurt and unsure of herself. Over those distressing first months she had often wondered whether she had been right or wrong in refusing Stephen's advances, whether it would have made any difference to his feelings for Samantha if she had given in to him. But she guessed not. It would only have made the situation worse as far as Brooke could see where she was concerned. At any rate, it was impossible to turn back the clock.

Two days later Stephen had taken one look at Samantha and fallen head over heels in love with her. At least, that was what he had tried to explain to Brooke in the note he left for her. He said he found he couldn't go through with the wedding feeling as he did for Samantha. So Stephen and Samantha had left together a week before the wedding without telling anyone where they were going. There was just the short note for Brooke from Stephen saying he was sorry and that he hoped she would understand.

Brooke felt her heart contract, recalling the moment she had opened Stephen's letter. Her parents had been absolutely flabbergasted, hardly able to believe it had happened. Brooke's brother Mike, two years her junior, had gone angrily in search of Stephen, but he had taken Samantha interstate. She hadn't seen Stephen since that fateful weekend, although her aunt had written to say that Stephen and Samantha had married quietly and were living somewhere in Victoria where Stephen was teaching in a private school.

Brooke studied Stephen's face and then replaced the photograph in the drawer where it had lain for nearly a year. The pain she usually felt when she allowed herself to think of him had faded somewhat, leaving only the dull ache of rejection mingled with something she was loath to admit was wounded pride. Switching out the light, she climbed back into bed, stretching her arms behind her head and staring into the gloom. If she was honest with herself she would admit that she had built Stephen and their relationship into something totally unrealistic, and she recognised the making of that admission as the first major step forward she had taken in the whole year.

Kath was right. She had let herself go to seed, and for what? She smiled grimly at her turn of phrase, picturing herself in a garden like a forgotten lettuce. Perhaps her sense of humour hadn't died either.

Once she had prided herself in her appearance. She knew she wasn't a beauty by any means, but she had been attractive. And she would be again. What she needed was a complete change. At the time, her mother had suggested she transfer to another school, get away from old memories of Stephen, but she had stubbornly refused to consider it, preferring to stay and face the whole thing head on. Well, a year was long enough proof of her staying power. She would move on to, she hoped, greener pastures.

Firstly, she would see the principal at school and ask to be considered for a transfer—anywhere in Queensland would do. And her appearance, that needed immediate attention. She'd phone the hairdresser's and have her hair cut and styled. She'd even have the full beauty treatment. It was a long time since she had pampered herself. This weekend she would go through her clothes—yes, even her trousseau which had remained packed away out of sight because she hadn't even been able to bear looking at it. Some of the clothes were fairly basic styles which would not be unfashionable, so it would just be a matter of deciding what to keep and what to discard. She knew she had lost a little weight, but that was all to the good. She could easily alter the clothes herself. In fact, she would even treat herself to a few new outfits.

It was time the staid old Miss Drynan changed her outlook. She was only twenty-five years old, after all, hardly in her dotage. There were plenty of years ahead of her, God willing, to make a full and satisfying life for herself. A young life, not the cold, shallow world she had existed in for the past year.

With all these plans firmly made, as she turned over and fell into a peaceful and satisfying sleep, she decided she must remember to thank Kath and Jilly and Barbara for shaking her out of her emotional exile.

If Brooke's parents were surprised when she announced that she had applied for a transfer to another school they tried hard not to show it. It was a few days later and she had spoken to her principal, who had reluctantly promised to try to arrange the transfer for her, irregular though it was in the middle of the school year.

'Where are you likely to be transferred to?' asked her eighteen-year-old sister Renee. 'You don't mean outside of Brisbane, do you?'

'It could be anywhere from here to the Birdsville Track,' laughed Brooke.

'Who, in their right mind, that is, would want to go there?' retorted fourteen-year-old Craig. 'You'd frizzle up into an old dragon overnight!'

'Thanks very much,' replied Brooke, with feeling. 'Because it's not the usual time for transferring I'll have to go wherever there's a vacancy, as though I was on the relieving staff like Jilly Martin. I don't really mind where it is, although I know I'll miss you all if I do have to leave home.'

'I think the change will do you good,' said her brother Mike. 'You could get posted out into the country and you might pick up a rich cow cockie; those cattlemen are always well heeled; or maybe a cane farmer who'll make it his business to support your favourite brother for the rest of his life. I always fancied retiring early,' he winked at Brooke.

'I can't see you leading an idle life somehow, Mike,' laughed Brooke.

'Gosh, you know how much I've always wanted a horse of my own,' said Craig, who had been giving the matter careful thought, 'so make it a cow cockie, Brooke. Tell you what, I'm a bit browned off with my school, too, so I'll transfer with you. I can look after you, see you don't get into any trouble. What do you say?' he appealed to his sister.

The rest of the family raised their eyes skywards.

'That's just what Brooke needs, a troublesome little brother tagging along, cramping her style,' stated Renee, pulling a face at Craig. 'More than half an hour with you would be enough to drive her around the twist,' she added with sisterly candour.

'Perhaps you should try to give the work at your present school more of your attention before you head further afield, young man,' said their father, smiling at Craig's disgruntled expression.

'How come everyone has to treat me like a little kid? You know, if we had a bigger family I wouldn't be the youngest, then you'd have someone else to pick on,' said Craig.

'Heaven forbid!' said his mother with feeling.

Two days before the end of the second school semester Brooke was summoned to the principal's office. There were a couple of positions waiting to be filled in Charters Towers in north Queensland. She would be replacing one of the teachers whose health had suffered in the hot tropical climate and, if she accepted the position, the flat which the previous teacher had occupied would be kept for her. She tossed over in her mind all she knew about Charters Towers. It was a city, inland from Townsville, and used to be a major goldmining centre. Brooke allowed herself little time to ponder over the decision. All at once, the idea that she could travel to the tropical north of her state, break new ground, was just what she needed to make her fresh start. Besides, the principal had also informed her that Jilly

Martin had been given notice that she would be relieving in Charters Towers, so it wasn't as though she would be entirely on her own.

Brooke hurried back to her classroom, her mind spinning and her tummy full of butterflies. Her transfer was virtually through and she was all but on her way, she thought, excitement adding a lift to her steps, her newly styled shoulder-length hair rippling in soft waves about her face. She had an urge to run along the corridor and wondered what the students would think if they saw the very proper Miss Drynan skipping along the verandah like a six-year-old. She suppressed a giggle at the picture she conjured up and realised she hadn't felt so alive in ages.

'What's come over you, Brooke Drynan? I even heard a rumour about a transfer.' Kath Barton dropped a stack of textbooks on her desk in the staffroom.

Her friend looked up and smiled half apologetically. 'Hasn't anyone around here heard the old saying "loose lips sink ships"? I didn't know about the transfer myself until two hours ago.'

'Seriously, Brooke, are you really going to leave us?' frowned Kath.

'Yes, I guess so.' Brooke propped one elbow on her desk and rested her chin on her hand. 'Leaving my family and friends will be a wrench, but I think the time has come for me to make the break. I've been here for four and a half years now and—well, what with one thing and another, I'm in a bit of a rut, a very comfortable and pleasant rut but a rut for all that. I'm finding I like the world again and I need the change now, Kath, before it's too late to take the first step. I'm starting the new semester in Charters Towers.'

Kath raised her eyebrows. 'Charters Towers? But why so far away? You'll positively melt up there, Brooke! It's practically the back of beyond. In fact, it's so far past the Black Stump I bet the people there haven't even heard of it, let alone seen it.'

Brooke chuckled at Kath's description of the north.

'That was the only vacancy at the moment. It was a case of take it or leave it, so I jumped at it.' Brooke's eyes sparkled. 'I'm replacing Frank Dennis. He wasn't in our year, was he?'

'Don't recall the name,' Kath replied, and was thoughtfully silent for a moment. 'You know, Brooke, I came in here all fired up to try to talk you out of leaving. I didn't think much of the idea of you breaking away, but now I'm not so sure I would have been right to try to change your mind, even if I could have done so. I think I see the light and I can understand why you need the change. I get the feeling that you're pretty excited about the whole thing. Your face is alive again, and I'm just so glad to see it. I was beginning to despair of you, to tell you the truth, I really was.'

'I know,' Brooke grinned impishly. ' "Brooke, you're turning into a frump",' she mimicked her friend's voice.

'Oh, Brooke, no!' Kath's face flamed. 'You didn't. . . .?'

'Overhear you? Yes, I did, and I want to thank you all for caring enough to want to do something about me. I guess I was so busy showing everyone how brave I was to carry on that I almost forgot that living meant more than just eating, sleeping, and breathing. I have a feeling I was developing into a rare old pain in the neck,' grimaced Brooke, and they both laughed.

'Hardly that,' said Kath.

Brooke sighed. 'Well, my decision is made and I'm burning most of my bridges. I'm really looking forward to the next semester, Kath. It's a challenge for me—new town, new school, new people, and suddenly, that's just what I need. Getting used to a new group of students should keep me on my toes.'

'You could say that,' said Kath drily. 'We're sure going to miss you, Brooke. The old place won't seem the same at all. And wait until the guys hear about your transfer.' She laughed. 'I'll never forget the look on

Garth Warren's face when you turned up with your hair cut and styled, minus your glasses and all, decked out in that great red and white sundress. I thought his eyes would roll on to the floor!'

'He did seem at a loss for words for once,' Brooke chuckled, 'but he recovered soon enough to ask me out for a drink.' She shook her head. 'He's really incorrigible. Be sure to warn my replacement about Mrs Warren and the four little Warrens.'

'What's that about old Warren the Wolf?' asked Jilly Martin, bouncing into the staffroom and throwing herself into her chair. 'You've certainly shaken him right down to his flirtatious roots, Brooke. In the last couple of days he's been following you everywhere.'

'I was just telling Kath to be sure to warn the replacement against him,' said Brooke.

Jilly sat up. 'What replacement? Who's leaving besides me?'

'Brooke is,' replied Kath. 'Didn't you hear the rumour?'

'No.' Jilly looked at Brooke in amazement. 'I've been on a cross-country with some third-formers and never heard a word. I'm always the last to find out what's going on, you know that. What's brought all this on, Brooke? It's not usual to be transferred mid-year. I mean, I'm on the relieving staff so I can expect to be transferred at the drop of a hat, in fact, I have been, but that hardly applies to you. Did you complain to the principal about it?'

Brooke shook her head. 'No, Jilly, I asked for the transfer, so I'm beginning the next semester in Charters Towers with you. Looks like you can't get away from me!'

It was Jilly's turn to be momentarily at a loss for words. 'You mean we're both going up to the Towers?' Her face broke into a broad grin. 'Brooke, that'll be great! But are you sure you want to go so far away? What about the heat and the dust and the flies? I spent most of my childhood in the north and I've stayed with relatives all over the place up there, so I know what to expect and, believe me, the heat's supposed to get to you after a while,' she said seriously, 'sends you troppo!'

Kath and Brooke both burst out laughing.

'I'll soon acclimatise,' said Brooke. 'Besides,' she glanced at Kath, who grinned sheepishly back, 'I've turned over a new leaf and I wanted a change to go with it.'

'Mmm.' Jilly looked quickly at Kath and then thoughtfully back at Brooke. 'When you put it like that I see what you mean. And it's about time your tree started with the new leaves,' she added cryptically. 'Well,' she raised her hands in a gesture of concession, 'if we can't talk you out of it the next best thing is to turn my farewell party into our farewell party. Saturday night at my place? Sharing a house has definite advantages when it comes to holding a wing-ding. We'll have a barbecue in the back yard. Now,' Jilly grabbed a notebook, 'let's see what we're going to need. We'll invite the staff and their wives, husbands, friends or whatever,' she began.

Brooke and Kath looked helplessly at each other, knowing how hard it was to restrain Jilly when she fell to organising.

The combined farewell party turned into something of a marathon, in volume and duration. It continued until the early hours of Sunday morning and filled Jilly's backyard to capacity. Everyone seemed to be having a great time, even Brooke, who had felt a little ill at ease about the whole thing, not having mixed with people much at all since her break-up with Stephen.

The party was in full swing and it was about halfway through the evening, when Brooke had successfully parried the amorous advances of Garth Warren, that Jilly led, with more than a little difficulty, a new arrival through the throng of people, to introduce him to

Brooke and her mother.

Dave Martin was a cousin of Jilly's and Brooke put his age at about thirty or perhaps a little older. Jilly informed them that he was a fellow teacher.

'I've done some more arranging, Brooke,' Jilly was saying confidently, and Dave made a grimace in Brooke's direction.

'That's nothing new for Jilly,' he grinned apologetically. He had a nice open face, curling black hair, and his grin was cheerfully infectious. 'Jilly's family nickname is "tidal wave". She sweeps everything and everyone before her without a by your leave, so don't feel obliged to agree to any of it if you aren't completely happy about the arrangements.'

Brooke had decided she liked Dave and his friendliness put her instantly at ease. 'What plans now, Jilly? Tell me the worst,' she laughed.

'Nothing earth-shattering, honestly, Brooke. Last night I happened to ring my aunt, Dave's mother, in Townsville, to see if she'd mind if we called in to see her on the way through to the Towers, and she gave me some interesting information. As luck would have it, who do you think has also been banished to the far north? None other than my favourite cousin David here,' explained Jilly. 'And who do you think has a car which has packed it in and therefore needs a lift up to Charters Towers?'

'None other than Cousin David,' finished Dave with resignation.

Brooke's mother was glancing perplexedly from one to the other.

'I thought you'd be happier about Brooke and me driving up north together if you knew we had some impressive company in the form of this tall and strong Adonis to protect us instead of us driving all that way on our own,' Jilly beamed at Mrs Drynan and turned back to her cousin. 'Show your muscles, Dave.'

'Jilly always has to have the drama,' said Dave, turning to Brooke's mother. 'What Jilly meant to say, Mrs Drynan and Brooke, was that as my car needs major repairs I would appreciate a lift up north and would be quite prepared to share expenses with the girls. That is, if Brooke has room in her car for an extra person and his suitcase.' He looked at Brooke. 'It would only be as far as Townsville where my parents live, although I've been transferred to the same school as you and Jilly.'

'Well, what do you say, Brooke?' asked Jilly.

Before Brooke could comment her mother broke in. 'I think it sounds a very good idea for everyone,' Mrs Drynan said firmly.

'I must admit I was a little worried about Brooke and Jilly heading off alone to drive over sixteen hundred kilometres. Some of the areas are so isolated and one hears such shocking things befalling young women these days. I know your father will be very pleased for you to have Jilly's cousin along.'

'There, what did I tell you, Dave?' said Jilly. 'That works out fine. Just leave everything to good old Jilly. I must say I like the ends to be tied. Well, I'll leave you and Dave to get acquainted,' she finished, and headed towards a group of younger members of the gathering who were seated around the record player and were being held responsible for the frenzied sounds issuing forth from that piece of equipment.

Mrs Drynan went off in search of her husband to inform him of the latest developments, leaving Brooke and Dave together to 'get acquainted', as Jilly put it. And get acquainted they did. The more Brooke talked to Jilly's cousin the more she liked him. He had an ever-ready sense of humour which wasn't in the slightest malicious and they chatted away as though they had known each other for years.

Dave taught manual training subjects, he told her, woodwork, metal work, technical drawing, etc., and Brooke could tell that he genuinely enjoyed his work. He had lived all his life in Townsville, but he had had a touch of itchy feet and moved down to Brisbane where he had been teaching for three years. Now he felt the urge to return to his home in the north of the state.

When the vacancy at the Charters Towers State High School had cropped up, Dave had been quick to accept it as he had been waiting for a transfer up north for over six months and had resigned himself to waiting until after the Christmas break. As Charters Towers was only one hundred and thirty-five kilometres inland from Townsville he could drive home to be with his family every weekend if he so wished. As far as Dave was concerned his move could only have been bettered had he been transferred to Townsville itself. Apparently he had friends in Charters Towers with whom he was going to board.

Jilly returned some time later, a frown puckering her brow. 'I've been nattering to Joe Donovan, who teaches at Salisbury High, and it seems he's a friend of that Dennis fellow you're replacing, Brooke. And to cut a long story short he says that Frank Dennis had to be transferred because he couldn't cope with the students.'

'What, all of them?' asked Brooke. 'Any idea how big the school is?'

'About four hundred students, I'd reckon,' said Dave. 'It's pretty small as secondary schools go. But I wouldn't worry too much, sometimes a guy just clashes with an element in one class.'

'Joe Donovan says they've had four replacements including this Frank Dennis. There's three of us, so it sounds pretty fishy to me. Maybe this element of yours is actually a school full of plain out-and-out little louts, Dave,' said Jilly.

'Well,' Brooke shrugged her shoulders resignedly, 'surely there'll be one or two little saving graces in the bunch. I don't think it's going to be dull somehow, by the sound of it, do you, Jilly?'

'Dull? Charters Towers? Never!' said Jilly, her eyes flashing. 'Those who have passed on have just turned in their graves. The Towersites are proud of their rip-roaring heritage,' she laughed. 'Actually, I'm looking forward to going back to my old stomping ground. Although I haven't taught there, I spent part of my schooldays in the Towers, just like Dave. Wow!' A thought suddenly struck her. 'I'll have another chance at Kley MacLean!' She clasped her hands together and raised her eyes skywards. Dave burst out laughing and Jilly joined in.

'Who's this Kley MacLean?' Brooke smiled enquiringly at them when their laughter abated.

'He's divine! The King of the Cattle Country,' Jilly told her. 'I hope he hasn't been snared by some scheming female, has he, Dave?'

'Who, Kley? Not him! He's our last citadel. If he's stormed the whole lot of us mere males go down with him,' laughed Dave. 'He's a dyed-in-the-wool bachelor who'll never get hooked, you can take it from me. Oh, he's not exactly anti-women, just thinks they should know their place.'

'Good grief! He sounds like he should live in a cave and carry a club,' retorted Brooke.

'Take no notice of him, Brooke,' said Jilly. 'Wait till you meet him. He's got everything. Dave's one of his best friends, so we have an ideal means of association. I met him about—oh, three years ago when I spent a holiday in Townsville with Dave's parents and I'd like to renew the acquaintance. Mmmm! Tall, dark, handsome, rich. Brooke, you'll fall for him immediately, take my word for it.'

'I dislike him immensely already,' Brooke wrinkled her nose. 'If there's one thing I can't stand it's an arrogant, conceited, self-opinionated "Lord of the Manor" who expects to have his adoring harem hanging on his every word.'

This statement had Dave laughing again. 'Oh, Brooke,' he took a breath, 'I can't wait to see Kley's face when you tell him that!'

'Humph!' Brooke remarked deprecatorily.

'Just you wait and see, Brooke,' said Jilly, smiling knowingly. 'He's absolutely dangerous to a girl's equilibrium. None of us are immune to his charm.'

'There's always an exception to every rule,' said Brooke primly, causing Dave and Jilly more merriment.

By the time the party eventually broke up the arrangements for their journey north had been made and all that remained was for Dave to phone Jilly to verify their estimated time of departure on the following Wednesday. Brooke and Jilly had decided to share the flat which had been vacated by Frank Dennis and his wife so they would have a week to sort themselves into some order before the first day of the next school semester.

CHAPTER TWO

BROOKE's little blue sedan purred along Highway One, eating up the eighty-eight kilometres between Ayr and Townsville. They had crossed the Burdekin River via the 'Silver Link', a bridge joining the twin towns of Homehill and Ayr which were only eleven kilometres apart. Dave explained that, including the approach spans, the bridge was over a thousand metres in length and that the structure of the bridge was most unusual in that huge concrete caissons had been sunk into the riverbed to a depth of thirty metres to carry the bridge, as there was no solid rock foundation.

As she looked at the wide expanse of sand and scattered shallow potholes of water, it was hard for Brooke to imagine that the river could become a raging torrent. She knew that the Burdekin Basin, covering an area of nearly thirty thousand square kilometres, was the biggest river watershed in the state. In several inland centres the river's waters were harnessed to provide power and water for the pastoral industry as well as crop irrigation. The Burdekin River Delta had been systematically tapped to provide irrigation from an unfailing reserve of underground water for rice crops, tobacco fields, tropical fruits and vegetables and beef cattle pastures, as well as the inevitable sugar cane.

Indeed, the prosperity of the area was obvious in the acre upon acre of green-topped, swaying sugar cane which stretched for kilometres along the roadside. The sugar crop, the area's major industry, also made its presence felt in the sickly sweet odour that drifted on the breeze. When Brooke remarked on it Jilly wrinkled her nose and told the other girl that she should smell it at the height of the season when the crops were burnt, harvested and processed, it was much worse then.

Soon they would be at the Martin home. Dave and Jilly had shared the driving with Brooke and they had made good time without pushing the little four-cylinder car beyond its limit.

They had spent the night before in Marlborough, one hundred kilometres north of Rockhampton, the town situated astride the Tropic of Capricorn and, although it had still been light when they reached Marlborough, Dave had suggested they stay the night there and tackle the two hundred and ninety kilometres to Mackay in the early morning. Night driving was always hazardous owing to the dangers of hitting straying cattle or kangaroos dazzled by the car's headlights. Jilly and Brooke had been only too glad to call it a day and Brooke was thankful that she had not had to make the journey on her own.

Jilly closed the door of the motel room she was sharing with Brooke. Dave had just returned to his own room after drinking a final cup of coffee with the girls. 'Poor Dave!' she sighed.

Brooke looked up from her suitcase at Jilly's quiet words. 'Why "Poor Dave", Jilly? He seems to be a very sensible, well adjusted fellow to me.'

'He puts on a good front, I'll give him that,' said Jilly, discarding her brunchcoat and throwing herself on to her bed in a very unladylike manner, 'but it must be hell for him going back.'

'Why so?'

'I don't suppose he told you why he left Townsville in the beginning, did he?' Jilly settled herself comfortably.

Brooke shook her head. 'He said he had itchy feet.'

'And a wrecked marriage.' She watched the expression of surprise cross Brooke's face. 'I hope he knows what he's doing, returning to the scene of the crime, so to speak. As far as I know he's still married. I didn't like to ask him and rake it all up, but I somehow can't see Dave filing for divorce. However, Jacqui may have. He was really besotted by that . . . that little bitch.'

Brooke raised her eyebrows at Jilly's strong descriptions.

'Actually, Dave met her when she was going out with Kley and when she found she couldn't have him she turned to Dave—at least that's how I read it. They were married Dave's first year out of college. I guess what it all boiled down to was that Dave wanted a wife and family and Jacqui wanted a career. She owns a little boutique in Townsville, very prosperous, I'm sorry to say. Dave's a nice fellow and I'm fond of him. He deserved better than the merry dance Jacqui led him. But I guess he's old enough to know what he's doing.'

'What did this Kley MacLean think of Dave taking his girl?' asked Brooke.

'Oh, Kley wouldn't have been all that cut up. He can have anyone he wants, and he rarely takes a girl out more than a couple of times. Mmm, but I bet those few times are pure bliss!' Jilly laughed as Brooke's face took on her best disgusted look. 'Time will tell,' she shook her finger at Brooke and then stiffled a yawn. 'Gee, I'm bushed! Travelling is so tiring and we've the worst part ahead of us tomorrow.'

Brooke turned down her bed and slipped beneath the light covers. She wouldn't have picked Dave Martin as being married—but then again, you never could tell. It was a pity. Dave was such a nice man and he would have been the last person she would have thought would have had marriage problems. He seemed so even-natured and easy-going. Perhaps the three years he had spent away from Townsville had given him time to come to terms with it. She sighed and settled deeper into her comfortable bed, trying to ignore the sensations of movement she was experiencing after driving all day.

Things like that always seemed to happen to really nice men, she thought sleepily, while others seemed to lead a charmed life with the whole world falling in place for them. Like that revolting friend of Dave's, Kley something or other. Her eyelids drooped and she fell asleep immediately.

They were up at dawn and started along the section of road which was previously known as the 'horror stretch', owing to its lack of habitation and the state of the road surface. However, the latter proved to be relatively good and, although the countryside was repetitive in its type of vegetation and topography, Brooke thoroughly enjoyed her first look at the tropics.

Now Dave was driving and they were joining the local traffic within the city of Townsville. Dave pointed out the landmarks with all the enthusiasm of homecoming as he drove down Flinders Street so that Brooke could take a look at the main city thoroughfare. She was enchanted by the wide streets with cool green palms growing along the centre strip, and as the sun was low in the sky and the shops and businesses were closed they could drive slowly enough for Dave to point out various buildings.

Eventually he turned out of the main traffic area in the direction of Castle Hill which ruggedly dominated the city's skyline. Brooke could pick out houses perched on the sides of the craggy hill, and it seemed that Dave was heading for one of these as they began to climb the winding road. However, about a third of the way up he turned along a narrow street and pulled the car to a halt in the drive of a beautifully kept high-set home.

Verandahs ran around three sides and the underneath of the house had been battened in, making a huge, airy entertainment area, which continued out the back into the hillside. The house was not new, but Brooke loved its tropical colonial design.

'Welcome to our place, Brooke,' grinned Dave, as a short plump grey-haired woman hurried down the stairs, her face wreathed in smiles.

Dave turned and enveloped his mother in a bear-hug, swinging her off her feet.

'David, put me down,' she gasped, 'you'll do yourself an injury throwing me about!'

Laughingly Dave planted his mother firmly back on

the ground after giving her a very noisy kiss. Jilly stretched thankfully and greeted her aunt affectionately while Dave drew Brooke forward.

'Mum, this is Brooke Drynan, who so kindly delivered me home.'

Brooke smiled shyly at Mrs Martin and to her surprise was folded in the older woman's arms and given a kiss on the cheek.

'Welcome to Townsville, Brooke. We've heard so much about you from Dave,' she said.

Brooke looked across at Dave in surprise.

'Mum exaggerates, as you'll realise when you get to know her better.' He shrugged his shoulders and grinned. 'One letter and one phone call, I assure you.'

'Well, come on upstairs and we'll have a nice cup of tea,' Mrs Martin shooed them towards the house. 'I've made you one of your favourite fruit cakes, Dave. I'm so pleased you've arrived safely. Were the roads all right? Last time your father and I drove down to your Aunt Sarah's in Mackay they were atrocious. That would have been just after that month of depressing rain we had, so I guess the wet weather accounted for the potholes and washouts, but I'll tell you, I was a nervous wreck by the time we got home. Your father was quite irritable with me, although why I don't know. I was only warning him of the rough bits in case he didn't see them. There now, sit yourselves down here and I'll have the tea brewed in no time.'

'You haven't changed a bit, Mum,' teased Dave, 'you could still talk the leg off an iron pot.'

'Get away with you, David,' chided his mother, 'you're as bad as your dad!'

'Where is Uncle John?' asked Jilly, getting a quick word in while her aunt drew breath.

'He had a late job this afternoon. He promised a young couple their house would be ready for the weekend and he's finishing it today instead of tomorrow. He'll be home any minute now. He's looking forward to seeing you, Dave, and having you home again,' Mrs

Martin turned from the bench where she was heaping
generous slices of homemade fruit cake on to a large
plate. 'We missed you so much.' Her eyes misted.

'You'll probably wish me back down south after a
few weeks,' Dave laughed a little selfconsciously as his
mother gave him another squeeze.

Jilly took the plate of cake out of her aunt's free hand
as it wobbled precariously.

'Do you know, Brooke, you may not think it now to
look at him, but our David took three first prizes in
baby shows before he was two years old,' smiled his
fond mother.

Brooke couldn't suppress a laugh at the expression
on Dave's face.

'And he's still pretty cute, Aunt Connie,' said Jilly,
setting her cup back on its saucer as she collapsed with
mirth. 'There are at least half a dozen females whose
hearts were left slightly bent when they learned that
Dave was leaving Brisbane.'

'Okay, enough's enough,' said Dave, a little pink
about the ears.

By the time Dave's father had arrived home Brooke
felt as though she had known the Martins for years.
They were certainly a wonderful family and obviously
thought the world of one another, making her feel a
pang of homesickness for her own family which she had
so recently left.

Mr Martin was an older edition of his son, only
much more taciturn. He shook hands solemnly with
Brooke and his tanned face, bearing the weathered
stamp of an Australian outdoorman, creased into a
slow smile. When he spoke he chose his words carefully,
only saying what he had to say. Dave had already told
Brooke that although his mother had been born in the
United Kingdom, both his parents had spent their child-
hoods and early married life in the station country in
the interior of the state.

They were soon discussing all the happenings of the

district, pausing every so often to explain various people and places to Brooke so that she wouldn't feel left out of the conversation. In next to no time they had broken down her natural reserve and she found herself relaxing in their undemanding company and joining in as though she were one of the family.

After dinner Brooke insisted on helping Mrs Martin with the dishes, leaving Jilly free to telephone her parents in Hughenden, which was two hundred kilometres west of Charters Towers.

'I hope having me stay the night isn't going to be too much trouble, Mrs Martin?' Brooke asked worriedly, thinking the Martins might prefer to make Dave's homecoming a family affair.

'Not in the least. Don't you give it another thought,' smiled Mrs Martin, swishing her washcloth about in the sudsy water. 'We've stacks of room, as you can see. This is a big old house and it's nice to have it occupied again. A house like this needs children's voices to take away the emptiness.' She looked wistful. 'Dad and I had hoped by now to have some grandchildren about, but,' she sighed 'it wasn't to be. Anyway,' she smiled, 'I'm just so pleased that Dave, and Jilly for that matter, have had such nice company on the trip up here. If all of Dave's friends in Brisbane are as nice as you are I can see I've been worrying unnecessarily. Not that I don't trust our Dave, mind,' she waved her dishcloth about, 'but you hear such terrible things these days, what with drugs and road accidents, etc.' She shook her head, reminding Brooke of her own mother.

'Well, actually, I haven't known Dave long,' began Brooke, feeling slightly guilty, 'but I went through college with Jilly. She arranged our meeting as Dave was coming up here as well.'

Mrs Martin nodded. 'That Jilly is certainly a livewire. I don't know where she gets her energy and that's a fact. Do you know, when Jilly gets started I can't get a word in edgeways, she's such a chatterbox. Goes from one subject to another without a breath.'

'And for anyone to get the better of Mum in the talking stakes is no mean feat,' grinned Dave, leaning in the kitchen doorway. 'If Jilly's father wasn't Dad's brother I'd say for sure she'd inherited her loquaciousness from you, Mum.'

'Stop your teasing, Dave. You'll be giving Brooke the wrong impression.' She turned back to rinse out the sink. 'There, that didn't take us long. Now, Brooke, I'll put these few dishes away and you go out on to the verandah with Dave and sit in the cool breeze. It's lovely out there of an evening. We get a breeze straight off the ocean and there's a nice view of Magnetic Island even at night. Off you go now. I'll join you in no time.'

The refreshing coolness on the verandah was delightful after the humidity of the day and Brooke felt pleasantly content watching the moonlight playing on the large island and the surrounding Pacific Ocean. She sighed happily.

'Enjoying our view, Brooke?' Dave's father broke the silence, filling his pipe with strong brown fingers.

She nodded. 'If I had this view I'd spend most of my time out here on the verandah. It's beautifully peaceful and relaxing.'

Mr Martin lit his pipe and nodded his agreement.

'Apart from the occasional cyclone,' murmured Jilly sleepily from her sprawling position on a folding lounge. 'Not that they're all so bad, but I never want to experience one like Althea a few years ago. Gosh, I was terrified! We all were. And the damage, you wouldn't believe it, Brooke.'

Mrs Martin joined them at that moment as the telephone rang and, with a sigh, she returned to the hall to answer it. Listening to the murmur of Mrs Martin's voice Brooke couldn't help thinking that whoever was on the other end of the line wasn't getting much of a word in, and she glanced at Dave, who laughingly said the same thing. Eventually his mother reappeared to tell an amused Dave that the call was for him. It was his friend Kley MacLean.

Brooke glanced across at Jilly, who winked outrageously. 'Just lead us to him,' she quipped. 'Our little joke, Aunt Connie,' she answered her aunt's raised eyebrows.

'Kley and Dave have been friends since they were boys,' Mrs Martin told Brooke. 'Kley's mother and I were distant cousins once or twice removed, and I guess you could say the boys have virtually grown up together, although Kley is a little older than Dave. Dave spent most of his school vacations on the MacLean cattle property or else Kley spent his holidays here with us. Dave and Kley were boarders at Thornburgh College in the Towers. The scrapes that Kley pulled our Dave out of, he was such a harum-scarum.'

'How are things on the Downs, Aunt Connie?' asked Jilly.

'Fine, just fine. It's a credit to Kley, that's for sure.' She turned to Brooke. 'The MacLean property is about fifty kilometres roughly north of Charters Towers, and a very good property it is, too. When his father died the responsibility for the entire outfit fell on Kley's shoulders and he was just turned eighteen. He certainly had to grow up quickly—too quickly really. I sometimes think he completely missed out on the best part of his youth,' she sighed. 'He worked that property like a grown man. That was, let's see—oh, it must be over fifteen years ago now. Old Fergus MacLean would have been so proud of him, wouldn't he, Dad?' she appealed to her husband, who nodded, his pipe between his teeth.

'As I told Kley when she called in a few days ago,' Mrs Martin, continued, 'it was time he was settling down and raising a family of his own. The girls of the district have had their eyes on him for years, all to no avail. He's never singled one out, much to the disappointment of lots of fond mothers,' she grinned merrily. 'We were only reminiscing about the good old days with Kley, weren't we, Dad?' Not waiting for confirmation from her long-suffering husband, she turned back to Brooke. 'You'll be able to meet him tomorrow night, Brooke. Dave had me get in touch with a few of his friends and have them come over for a get-together tomorrow evening. Luckily Kley was in town on business.'

'Oh, but I should get off to Charters Towers,' said Brooke quickly, 'I—that is, Jilly and I have to get settled into our flat.'

'Plenty of time for that,' dismissed Mrs Martin, waving one plump hand in the air. 'There's all next week before you go back to school. You must stay for the weekend at least.'

'As Aunt Connie says, plenty of time for all that,' Jilly drew lazily on her cigarette. 'Townsville's not a bad place. Dave and I will show you the sights and it will give us a break from the travelling. I don't know about you, Brooke, but my backbone will never be the same after two days of enforced sitting. I'm used to jogging around all day and I feel I'm about to seize up. Besides, you'd miss out on meeting Kley, and I can't wait to see that.'

Brooke completely ignored Jilly's baiting remark and addressed Dave's mother. 'I wouldn't dream of imposing on you,' she began.

'Now who said you were imposing? As I said before, we love having some young company about us, don't we, Dad? I don't remember there being one of Dave's friends we didn't like. Why, when our Dave first went down south to college I used to play some of his raucous records to stop myself going crazy in the peace and quiet.'

Dave rejoined them and lowered himself into an easy chair. Kley had phoned to confirm that Dave had arrived as planned and Dave had made sure he would be attending the party the next evening. 'I'm looking forward to catching up with Kley again, although he'll be a little late arriving tomorrow evening. He was telling me he was hoping to branch out into horse-breeding, Dad.'

They sat on the verandah chatting until Jilly yawned and stubbed out a second cigarette. 'That breeze is divine, but it's almost lulled me to sleep, so I think I might turn in.'

'An early night will do you all good,' clucked Dave's mother, 'especially with the party tomorrow night, so I'll leave you all to sleep in.'

As she relaxed in the comfort of the high-ceilinged old room Brooke decided that if the Martin family were any example of the people she was going to meet in North Queensland then she was sure she had made the right decision, that she was going to like it up here.

Although she hadn't planned on staying with the Martins for longer than one night she could hardly be churlish and insist that they push on tomorrow when Jilly was so keen on staying. After all, Jilly hadn't seen her relatives for some time. Brooke sighed. As they all said, there was plenty of time, so she might as well relax and enjoy it all and they were nice people.

Thoughts of the Martins began to merge into thoughts of Dave's friend, that paragon of virtue and answer to every maiden's prayer, Kley MacLean. Brooke frowned into the darkness. While Mrs Martin and Jilly were preparing another pot of tea Dave had told her a little more about his friend and the cattle property, Terebori Downs, which had apparently been in the MacLean family for over one hundred years. His father had been accidentally killed when thrown from his horse when Kley had been preparing to go to university in Townsville. With the death of his father, Kley had put these plans aside and taken on the running of Terebori Downs. She could imagine the strain of the responsibility that had been placed on the young Kley MacLean's shoulders, and although she could sympathise with him she was not looking forward to meeting him, no matter how attractive Jilly professed him to be.

Next evening Jilly had showered first and was down-stairs before Brooke was half ready. They had spent a restful morning, but during the afternoon Dave had them running around from one place to another gathering bits and pieces for the party. Jilly organised everyone in her own inimitable style. Brooke was consigned to Mrs Martin in the kitchen while Dave set up the chairs and tables for the food. Later the girls made a very passable effort of decorating the underneath of the house with streamers and balloons, and soon the area looked very partyfied.

As far as Brooke could ascertain from Dave—Mrs Martin and Jilly didn't seem to stand still long enough for Brooke to ask them—there would be about thirty or forty people coming. These were mainly Dave's friends along with two or three families of relations. And she was not overly upset that Kley MacLean would not be arriving until later in the evening.

By six-thirty Brooke had taken her turn in the shower and was seated at the solid old dressing table in front of a huge mirror applying her make-up. She lightly dusted her eyelids with pale mauve eyeshadow and then touched the tips of her curling lashes with a little dark mascara, thinking how different she looked without her heavy glasses. It seemed that the face in the mirror, anticipation of the party adding an attractive glow to her features, had shed at least five years since that night of truth in her bedroom when she had decided to change the direction of her life.

She grinned cheekily and winked at her reflection, laughing a little selfconsciously at herself as she reached for her dress and slipped into it, carefully easing it over her hips. Her dress had been one of her final purchases before she left Brisbane. The modern style in mauve Bombay featured a gathered lace-edged frill around the top which sat off the shoulders, leaving an expanse of creamy throat and shoulders bare. She hoped she wouldn't look too pale against the splendid suntans of the Northerners. The bodice beneath the frill gently moulded her firm breasts, emphasising her slim waist, and then the gathered skirt fell in mauve cascades about her long legs. As she pirouetted before the mirror the light material whirled softly against her skin.

She touched her full lips with pale lipstick and gave her hair a final brush. It fell to her shoulders with a suggestion of waves and flipped up nicely at the ends, the deep goldness of it shimmering under the bedroom light. Tonight she was going to enjoy herself. She felt young again. With a last critical look at her appearance she went downstairs to join the Martins.

Dave caught sight of her first and his expression showed momentary surprise. He recovered quickly and whistled appreciatively. 'Wow! What do you say about that, Dad?' he asked his father. 'I reckon we'll have to keep an eye on Brooke tonight. Can't have any of those tall good-looking friends of mine sweeping her off her feet, now can we?'

Mr Martin's face creased into a broad grin.

In brown tailored slacks and lemon shirt which set off his dark colouring, Dave looked quite handsome himself, and Brooke told him so. The last time she had seen him he had been dusty from head to foot from unloading the hired ice boxes for the beer and soft drinks. Now, with his curling dark hair brushed into order and his dark eyes dancing, she could see the attraction he would have for his opposite sex.

'You do look lovely, Brooke,' said Mrs Martin. 'It's a pleasant change to see young women in feminine dresses for a change instead of those jeans and scanty clinging tops.'

Dave winked at his father. 'Vive les scanty clinging tops!' He laughed and ducked a playful slap from his mother as the first of the cars pulled into the drive.

The entire group of guests seemed to arrive very punctually en masse, for soon the large area under the house was alive with people, laughing and talking over the background music from Dave's stereo outfit. Brooke was introduced to everyone, although she hadn't a hope of remembering half of their names. The majority of those attending the party were in their mid-twenties to early thirties, with a few younger relations and a couple of Dave's parents' contemporaries.

'Where's Kley?' at least four different girls asked in Brooke's hearing, and she could feel herself frown with irritation. Apparently there was no show without Punch up here in the north.

Not only was he the king-pin in Charters Towers, but it seemed his loyal subjects were scattered as far afield as Townsville. By the time he arrived she felt she would be hard pushed to be civil to him.

There was much laughter and the party continued in full swing. Mrs Martin arranged some strenuous and amusing games which everyone joined in with amused tolerance. Afterwards, the younger members began dancing to the beat music while the older people sat to the side and gossiped about their families and businesses or farms.

Thoroughly enjoying herself, Brooke was unaware that the inner pleasure she felt was reflected in her eyes to the extent that she had no lack of partners for the dances, so she danced and talked and laughed and began to feel a little lightheaded with the enjoyment of it all.

It was about ten o'clock when the party heralded a new arrival. At that particular moment Brooke was standing on a chair fixing a fallen streamer and a group of wayward balloons while Dave and Steve, one of Dave's young cousins, clasped her enthusiastically around the waist to 'keep her stable', as Dave put it. There was much laughter from the direction of the doorway, and from her high vantage point on the chair Brooke's gaze turned across the top of the heads of the crowd to see who had claimed everyone's attention. For

all the homage that was being paid to the newcomer it
had to be the Cattle King himself.

A tall dark man, with his back to Brooke, was hugging a laughing Mrs Martin to the obvious amusement
of the circle of onlookers. She let her gaze move over
what she could see of the man. He must have been well
over six feet tall and across the heads of Dave's milling
friends, as though he sensed her appraisal, a pair of
deep dark eyes encountered hers.

A quiver of awareness set her pulses pounding as
their eyes locked together and for one immeasurable
moment Brooke was powerless to break the spell. Then
those enigmatic eyes moved from her face, over her
figure with a practised ease, his gaze stopping momentarily on the two pair of hands still clasped about
her waist. Brooke felt her face flame with anger as his
gaze moved back to her face, his head rising arrogantly,
his eyes narrowing. Those eagle eyes hadn't missed a
thing, and if his cynically mocking expression was anything to go by it seemed that his assessment had found
her wanting.

Anger brightened her eyes as they clashed with his.
She flipped a strand of hair back behind her ear and
deliberately turned her best smile on Dave and Steve,
placing her hands on Dave's shoulders ready for him to
help her down, completely ignoring Kley MacLean. He
would find that not every girl came running and bowed
to pay homage. If the whole of north Queensland was
taken in by his lordly ways it didn't mean she had to
follow suit.

Brooke's brilliant smile was not lost on Dave and his
reaction was to lift her down into his arms, one arm
behind her knees and the other supporting her back,
and, still holding her against him, high off the floor, he
planted a light kiss on her lips.

She could almost feel the look of distaste from a pair
of dark eyes as the crowd parted and turned its attention on Dave's antics. Pink with embarrassment,

Brooke pushed her hand against Dave's chest.

'Dave, put me down——' she began. It was one thing to put on a show for the new arrival and another to be the centre of an enthusiastically cheering crowd. 'Dave!'

'Relax,' grinned Dave. 'Come and meet Kley.' And to her mortification he carried her through the crowd and deposited her right at the feet of the cattle baron.

CHAPTER THREE

'WHAT kept you, Kley?' asked Dave as the two men shook hands vigorously.

'You know how these meetings do go on.' His voice was deep and resonant and he turned his eyes back to Brooke. 'But had I known you'd invited such attractive friends I'd have closed the meeting earlier at all cost.'

The smile on his face did not match the mockery in his eyes and Brooke seethed with indignation. He was the most arrogant, conceited, self-opinionated. . . .

Dave laughed and drew her closer, one hand possessively on her waist. 'I shall probably regret it—but let me introduce you to Brooke Drynan, from the "Big Smoke". Brooke, this is Kley MacLean, who professes to be one of my best friends.'

Two can play at the same game, Mr High and Mighty MacLean, she thought, meeting his narrowed gaze. She'd met his type before. They expected every woman they met to fall all over herself to please. Well, he could jolly well prepare himself to meet his match!

She turned from Dave and, looking straight into Kley MacLean's mocking eyes, smiled her sweetest smile. 'Mr MacLean,' she breathed, her hand going out to him, 'how wonderful to meet you at last!' Her eyelashes fluttered. 'I've heard so much about you. You seem to be somewhat of a legend in these parts.' Her tone was only just derogatory, but she knew by the light flaring of his nostrils that her underlying taunting was not lost on him.

His mouth tightened angrily as he acknowledged the introduction with a slight inclination of his dark head and one large brown hand clasped hers firmly, sending vibrant signals along her nervous system. Those sparks

39

of tingling attraction were almost her undoing and she let her eyelids flutter down so that he would be unable to read the awareness in her widening eyes. When she looked up she had herself in control again.

From a distance his eyes had seemed to be dark brown, but up close she could see they were a deep dark blue, the whites clear and bright, and fringed by thick dark lashes. His dark hair, the ends bleached a shade lighter by the sun, was combed tidily in place, but it appeared to have a tendency to curl into disorder and the back was long enough to touch the collar of his crisp pale blue and whited striped shirt.

'You could say we've met already,' he said evenly, his eyes resting immovably on Brooke's face, and Dave looked enquiringly from one to the other.

'Across a crowded room,' he said mockingly, indicating the chair on which Brooke had been standing when he had arrived, the meaning behind his words bringing a blush to Brooke's cheeks.

The spark of awareness she had experienced at his first glance rekindled and with a shaky laugh she looked pointedly ruefully. 'Oh dear! And first impressions are so important.'

'You don't have to worry about first impressions on a male with twenty-twenty vision, Brooke,' laughed Dave. 'Your first impression is made for you, and very nicely too. Don't you think so, Kley?'

Kley inclined his head in that same arrogant way but refrained from commenting.

'Brooke can entertain you for a moment while I get you a drink,' said Dave, and to Brooke's horror, he moved away.

Alone with Kley MacLean, Brooke tensed as the other people nearby faded until, to her heightened senses, she was aware of only the tall dark man standing casually in front of her. Her first impulse was to flee, not to allow herself to be enmeshed in the web of his magnetism, for like it or not, she had to acknowledge that there was a magnetic quality about him. But then he was talking and the spell was broken, the world about her righted itself.

'What do you think of our northern hospitality, Miss Drynan, or are you revisiting our area?' He spoke with an exaggerated politeness, and although she had her eyes fixed somewhere on his shirt front she could feel his eyes were wandering appraisingly over her again, setting her aflame with the almost tangible sensation of his regard, and her anger returned to blaze anew.

Swallowing quickly, she hoped fervently that he was unaware of the conflicting effects his nearness was having on her. 'No. This is my first visit to the north,' she said, trying to sound offhand and ending up a little breathless. 'Dave's parents are wonderful people and I really appreciate their generous and kindly welcome. And please call me Brooke. I keep Miss Drynan for classroom use,' she smiled at him, amazing herself with her brazenness. The ball's in your court now, Mr Kley MacLean!

He was giving her the benefit of his penetrating gaze when Jilly erupted from the crowd.

'Kley!' she flung herself into his arms. 'I leave the room for two minutes and you slip in without my being here to welcome you properly!'

The tall man enveloped Jilly in his strong arms and kissed her enthusiastically. 'Jilly! Don't tell me you're back here as well. It's quite a gathering of the clan.' He was smiling broadly at the other girl.

Even from the side Brooke felt the force of that devastating smile, so she could understand Jilly's somewhat glazed expression. That spontaneous smile took years off his age as a deep line creased his tanned cheek and his full sensual lips lifted attractively.

'Something tells me you're still treating me like a nice little kid sister,' said Jilly ruefully. 'A brother like you is what I don't need. Who can match up to you?'

Kley's smile widened and his even white teeth flashed

against the darkness of his face. He tapped her playfully on the rear. 'You'll just have to keep looking, Jilly.'

Brooke schooled her features not to show her irritation at this exchange. Yes, she thought, she could see what Jilly had meant. To all outward appearances he had everything. He was tall, dark, attractive, but good looks were only part of the story where she was concerned. Stephen Marsh had been good-looking too. Anyway, why should she worry, she just wasn't interested.

The party-makers closed in on them again and Brooke managed to drift away from Kley's disturbing presence, although she suspected that one perfidious part of her wanted desperately to stay. But she labelled that thought as ridiculous and determined to put him firmly from her mind. This was easier said than done as he seemed to have become the vocal point of the evening, and it soon became disgustingly clear to Brooke that all the females at the party, irrespective of their age, appeared to gravitate towards him like moths to a flame. To her prejudiced eye, the fact that he was on good terms with as many of the men did not enter into her prejudgment.

In the crowd Brooke was able, by keeping her wits about her, to keep herself apart from him, although she gave up trying to overlook the fact that he was there. On a couple of occasions, usually when she was being whirled about by Dave or one of his friends, she caught his gaze on her through a break in the throng of people and with admirable self-control she succeeded in looking nonchalantly away.

However, she relaxed her guard for a few moments as she sat virtually in a corner catching her breath after an energetic bout of dancing. Her partner, Dave's young cousin Steve, had gone off to fetch her a much-needed drink. An unused paper plate served as an adequate fan and, closing her eyes, she waved it to and fro in front of her, welcoming the cooling breeze it created. With her other hand she lifted her hair from the back of her neck so that some of the breeze had a drying effect on her dampened skin.

When she opened her eyes he was there in front of her, handing her a glass of fruit juice. She put down the paper plate and her fingers trembled un-characteristically when they encountered his as she took the glass from him.

He sat down on a chair facing her. 'Steve volunteered to fetch some more ice, so I've been deputised to bring your drink over.'

'Thank you, Mr MacLean.' She took a sip of the cool drink, striving to regain her self-possession which had been sadly unsettled by his sudden appearance. 'This is delicious, and I really needed it.' Her voice sounded almost normal. 'Dancing is a thirsty business,' she smiled.

He inclined his head in that same aloof manner. 'You seemed to be enjoying yourself.'

In her super-sensitivity where he was concerned she suspected his comment wasn't overly flattering and her hackles began to rise.

He paused for a few moments, his eyes moving to her throat, and she nervously let her hair fall back into place, clasping both hands around her frosty glass and feeling the throb of her pulse falter and begin an accelerated racing.

'Do you find the humidity tiring, coming from the cooler south?'

'Just a little. But I guess I'll get used to it.' She shrugged her shoulders, unaware that the movement set her hair swinging, turning it into a mass of shimmering gold lights. 'I suppose it can be rather hot out on your cattle station? Dave said it was a drier heat than it is here.'

Kley leant forward and rested his elbows on his knees, his hands clasped lightly together, and Brooke's pulse heat fluctuated disturbingly again. 'Yes, it is that.

It can be five degrees hotter inland and yet you would swear it was warmer here on the coast. You don't seem to feel it when the humidity's not as high.'

There was another silence, and not an easy one for Brooke. His nearness was almost suffocating, and the clean male odour of a tangy aftershave lotion wasn't helping her fight for composure either.

'By the way, it's Kley. I keep Mr MacLean for formal occasions.' His incredible blue eyes looked straight into hers and his face broke into a slow, absolutely devastating smile that caught Brooke rather like a blow to the solar plexis.

She had already started to smile back, in fact, she would have been hard pressed to stop herself, when she caught a slight flicker in those eyes. Good grief, that smile! It was his trump card, all set to charm her into submission, she realised with a shock that was almost as great as the original one she had experienced a moment earlier. He had sensed she hadn't been overcome by his previously infallible charm and his ego had been slightly dented. Now he was pulling out all stops to bring her to heel. The absolute nerve of the man! And she'd very nearly fallen for it, hook, line and sinker. It wouldn't do to underestimate this man, and she felt a quickening of excitement as she set about pitting her wits against him.

Surely she could be forgiven for being taken in by that smile for those few moments. There was no doubt it made him almost unbelievably attractive, softening the hard planes of his rugged face. Even now the after-effects of that heart-stopping smile on Brooke left her with an uneasy feeling twisting in the pit of her stomach and her legs felt so weak she knew they wouldn't have held her weight had she been standing.

But Kley was speaking again, and she forced herself to concentrate on what he was saying. 'Dave tells me the three of you are going on a tour of the city tomorrow.'

'Yes. Dave has suggested it,' she replied, relieved that they were on safer ground. 'He says there's a particularly good view of the whole city from the top of Castle Hill.'

'What's this, a huddle in the corner? Still a fast worker with the damsels,' teased Dave as he handed his friend a stubbie of ice cold NQ lager. 'Shove up, Brooke, love, I'm nearly dead on my poor feet!'

Kley's eyes went sharply from Dave to Brooke as she reluctantly shifted around one chair beside Kley. His denim-clad knee brushed hers and she had to school herself not to move away. Dave sat down and she was now caught between the two of them. She felt Dave's arm go around the back of her seat and his hand rested lightly on her bare shoulder, a fact that wasn't missed by the cold stare of his friend.

Jilly bounded up, when Brooke's nerves had stretched to screaming pitch, and she made the most of the empty seat on the other side of Kley, resting one elbow on his broad shoulder and looking teasingly into his eyes. Jilly was welcome to him, thought Brooke exasperatedly.

Meanwhile the conversation flowed without more than desultory help from Brooke and Kley. Not that any extra conversation was needed from anyone else when Jilly was holding the floor, and it wasn't until Dave's mother beckoned for the girls to help with the setting out of the supper that Brooke could make her escape.

'What do you think of him, Brooke?' asked Jilly.

'Who?' Brooke was deliberately obtuse.

The two girls were standing alone outside in the courtyard, getting a breath of fresh air.

'Brooke Drynan, you're teasing,' said Jilly. 'Kley MacLean. Who else?'

'Oh, he's all right,' Brooke's voice was offhand. 'The external wrapping is attractive enough, but I'm not so sure about what's inside.'

'Who cares what's inside? I wouldn't care if it was all

sawdust,' laughed Jilly. 'I could sit and look at him for hours.'

Booke laughed reluctantly.

'But truthfully now, Brooke, didn't your heart flutter just a tiny bit when you first saw him?' asked Jilly. 'I was mad as a hornet because I wasn't here to see you two come face to face.'

'I've told you, looks aren't everything. And I wouldn't go getting all fired up about the King and me if I were you, Jilly, because I'd say he's as totally unimpressed with me as I am with him,' she told Jilly quietly.

'Not from where I stand,' remarked Jilly. 'He couldn't keep his eyes off you. Oh, he wasn't that obvious,' she hastened to reassure Brooke when she noted her friend's shocked expression. 'But I've been watching him, I always watch him. He's pure poetry in motion,' she sighed, 'anyway, when he thinks you're not looking his eyes follow you.'

'Jilly, stop exaggerating!' A quiver of unbidden excitement stirred Brooke's senses.

'Would I lie to you, Brooke? About that gorgeous hunk of man?' demanded Jilly. 'I only wish he'd look at me like that. Just once.' She appealed to the starry heavens. 'You know, Brooke, I reckon you could have him just where you want him if you were interested. I've never noticed him react to a girl in this way before, and I think Dave's noticed it, too.'

'Well, I'm not interested, thank you very much.' Brooke looked at Jilly and a thread of an idea took formation in her mind. 'You really think I could attract his interest?' she asked, half to herself.

'I'm positive you could,' said Jilly.

'Mmm.' Brooke smiled wickedly. 'You know, it would jolly well teach him a lesson if I did.'

'What do you mean, teach him a lesson?' asked Jilly. 'I wouldn't have said he needed any lessons. I'd say he could probably teach us a few things.' She raised her eyebrows suggestively.

'Undoubtedly,' said Brooke drily. 'I mean it would serve him right if I led him up the garden path and then gave him some of his own back by telling him thanks, but no, thanks, he isn't my type.'

'That's not the Brooke Drynan I know speaking!' Jilly was shocked and then she laughed. 'You wouldn't do it, Brooke. You wouldn't have the nerve.'

'Oh, wouldn't I?' Brooke could just see his arrogant face when she put him in his place and the feeling made her lightheaded.

'Bet you a dollar you wouldn't,' Jilly challenged her.

'Oh, I don't know about betting, Jilly. It sounds sort of coldblooded.' Brooke began to regret her hasty words.

'No, come on, Brooke, have a go! You can't back out now. A dollar on it,' teased Jilly.

'All right—one dollar,' agreed Brooke recklessly. 'I'll use my wiles to cultivate his interest and when I have his undivided attention I'll tell him just what I think of arrogant, self-opinionated, egotistical he-men.'

'This I've got to see,' said Jilly, and her eyes widened as her eyes left Brooke's face and focused on something just past her.

Brooke turned to follow her gaze, her heart sinking, knowing just what she would see before her eyes told her he was standing there. Her face flushed and she swallowed helplessly. Had he overheard their conversation? She cringed inside, feeling cheap and nasty. If he had been attracted to her as Jilly suspected then her little speech would have killed that on the spot.

She couldn't hazard a guess at his thoughts from his face as it was completely expressionless, although she thought she caught a flash of steel in his eyes.

'Looking for us, Kley?' Jilly was first to find her voice, although she too was a little pink.

'One of your aunts is about to leave and she would like to say goodbye to you and Brooke,' he said evenly, and Brooke wondered if she had imagined the almost imperceptible pause before he had said her name.

As they moved back to the party proper Brooke suspected that even Jilly's light banter sounded a trifle forced.

By the time she crawled heavy-eyed into bed it was nearing two a.m., and although she expected to lie awake for ages after such an emotion-charged evening, she fell into an undeservedly dreamless sleep as soon as her head touched her pillow, before she could even begin to analyse the reason for Kley MacLean's disturbing attraction and the almost assured premonition that she was going to live to regret dearly her outrageous bet with Jilly.

'Are you ready to go, Dave?' asked Jilly, preparing to lever herself out of her comfortable chair, attractive in her brown shorts and embroidered cream blouse, the colours toning with her large brown eyes and dark hair and complexion.

Dave had joined the two girls on the verandah next morning, the keys of his father's car jangling in his hand. 'Just about. Kley should be here any minute,' he remarked, glancing at his watch.

Jilly stopped, halfway out of her chair, and Brooke's eyes widened with surprise almost bordering on horror.

'Didn't I mention that I'd invited Kley along?' Dave hit his forehead with the palm of his hand. 'I must have forgotten. The couple of drinks I had evidently addled my brain,' he grinned, looking from Jilly to Brooke. 'What's the problem? You can't not want to spend time with Kley? You remember Kley MacLean, Jilly, your idol of idols? Surely you can't have forgotten,' he laughed.

Jilly glanced quickly at Brooke and then laughed with Dave. 'Not me. I was simply momentarily at a loss for words at the thought of seeing him again so soon, that's all.'

Dave shook his head. 'Women! I'm going to back the car out,' he started down the steps. 'Come down when you're ready.'

As he disappeared around the corner of the house Jilly flopped back into her chair. 'Phew! That gave me quite a stir. Do you suppose Kley overheard anything last night, Brooke?'

'I'm not sure. I couldn't tell from his expression.' She frowned, her heartbeat pounding erratically. 'It depends on how long he'd been standing there.'

'It couldn't have been long or else I would have noticed him,' said Jilly without a lot of conviction.

'Well, I certainly hope he didn't hear anything,' said Brooke, and closed her eyes tightly for a moment. 'Oh dear, if he did, what must he be thinking of me? I'm so mad with myself. I can't think what came over me. Fancy even suggesting such a . . . a. . . .' She shook her head.

'Does that mean the bet's off?' asked Jilly, and held her hand up when Brooke turned towards her. 'Sorry, Brooke, just joking.'

They were both lost in thought for a moment.

'You know, I'm sure he couldn't have overheard us,' said Jilly finally. 'I still say you could do it too,' she grinned. 'It would be fun to try.'

'Oh, Jilly, you can't mean that,' said Brooke unhappily, and before she could say any more a pale blue Ford Fairlane drew up in front of the house. Brooke watched mesmerised as a dark head, followed by a tall well-built body, emerged from the driver's side.

'Come on, you two,' called Dave, and with one final questioning look at each other Jilly and Brooke walked downstairs to join the men.

A couple of times during their drive up the winding road to the top of Castle Hill Brooke caught her breath as the narrow road twisted around a granite outcrop in a hairpin bend. However, she had to admit that the view as they climbed upwards was spectacular. When they reached the summit Dave parked the car past the panoramic restaurant and they mounted the steps to the lookout.

Deciding discretion was the better part of valour,

Brooke had decided to play the whole day very low key. Her smile at Kley as he wished them good morning had been as calm and unassuming as she could manage, although she knew her colour had heightened noticeably.

He wore dark blue flared slacks and a pale blue lightweight knit shirt, its short sleeves moulding his muscular arms. In the bright unrelenting sunlight, he lost none of his attractiveness and, if possible, he was even more compelling.

His eyes met hers as he held open the rear door of the Statesman de Ville for her and he allowed his gaze to move downwards with deliberate slowness over her simply cut sundress, bare legs and neat white sandals. Brooke climbed hurriedly into her seat before he could see her blush crimson her face.

Now, from this highest vantage point, the three northerners took turns to acquaint Brooke with various sections of the city. The three-hundred-and-sixty-degree panorama of the entire city lay below them, the fleet of small craft moored in the safety of Ross Creek, the chequered patterns of houses in the suburbs, bisected here and there by a highway or railway line, the sparkling beaches stretching to the north and south, the turquoise Pacific Ocean reaching to the horizon with Magnetic Island dominating Halifax Bay while to the rear the Leichhardt and Hervey Ranges provided a backdrop for the entire tableau.

Screwing his eyes up against the sun's glare, Dave pointed out the Ross River Meatworks and the Copper Refinery which, he said, was a subsiduary of Mount Isa Mines Limited and the largest refinery of its kind in Australia. Being the centre of two opulent sugar lands, that of the Burdekin River Delta in the south and the Herbert River Valley to the north, the port of Townsville boasted a large bulk sugar terminal, he told Brooke, while also being an outlet for beef, wool and timber from the hinterland.

The Lavarack Army complex and the Garbutt R.A.A.F. Base, with half a dozen Neptune reconnaissance aircraft, used for maritime patrol, sitting on the tarmac, was set out below in miniature. Another cluster of buildings constituted the James Cook University which has become well known as its faculties specialise in the fields of veterinary and marine sciences related to the tropical environment.

Castle Hill, a granite peak, Dave told her, was approximately three hundred metres high and was also known as Mount Cutheringa, although in actual fact it was just short of being classed officially as a mountain, and its well-known shape made it a prominent landmark.

The journey down the hill proved even more scarifying than the drive up and Brooke was glad she was in the back right-hand side of the car beside Jilly so that she could admire the view without being able to see the drop beside the road at close quarters.

The remainder of the scenic tour took place on the relative flat of the city, and for Brooke the only jarring note was the studied watchfulness of a pair of blue eyes reflected squarely in the rear vision mirror. They walked through Anzac Park, admiring the beautiful tropical gardens where blooms provided vivid splashes of intense colour. In the car again they drove slowly along the Strand, an impressive boulevard on Townsville's foreshore, its green lawns, flowering trees and slender palms fringing the crystal clear waters of Halifax Bay. The Cliff Gardens Waterfall, an artificial cascade provided a cooling spectacle as it tumbled down between the hanging gardens of bougainvillea.

Their tour finished up on the banks of Ross Creek where they strolled along looking at the various motor-cruisers, yachts, catamarans and trimarans moored in the boat harbour. A large cruiser moored a short distance from the shore belonged to Kley. He used it mainly to motor across to Magnetic Island where he owned a holiday house, but he told Brooke he also had a weakness for deep sea fishing and went out as often as he was able to get away from the station.

'I'm going over to the island tomorrow, my young nephew is spending his school vacation on the island and I promised I'd go over when I came down to Townsville,' said Kley. 'Why don't you three come over with me? We could show Brooke over the island.'

'Sounds great to me,' replied Dave eagerly. 'We could do a bit of snorkelling, I really missed that down in Brisbane. Ever tried it, Brooke?'

'Well, no,' she replied, 'but I couldn't possibly go with you. I . . . we have to get to Charters Towers,' she appealed to Jilly for back-up, but the other girl was suddenly very interested in the nautical scene on the boat harbour. 'And it would mean another night at your place and I don't want to overstay my welcome.'

Dave waved that airily aside. 'That's no worry. Right, it's all settled. We'll all go over to the island in the morning. You'll love it, Brooke. We can swim and snorkel and walk along the reefs at low tide. Just like old times, Kley?'

Brooke opened her mouth to protest and closed it again. Jilly had the nerve to smile sympathetically and said quietly, 'It really is very nice over on Magnetic Island, Brooke. You'll enjoy it.'

Brooke donned her bikini and slipped into a pair of soft scrub denim shorts and a cool printed top. They were to meet Kley at the boat and Brooke didn't want to hold them up. Into her large carryall she shoved some underclothing, her beach towel, protective suntan lotion and a pair of jeans and a matching light jacket in case the weather turned cool on the journey home in the cruiser. She grabbed her sunglasses as Dave sounded the horn outside.

As they drove down to the boat harbour Brooke could feel within her a rising sense of dread mixed incomprehensively with a flicker of anticipation. That both the dread and the anticipation were closely associated with the one object, one Kley MacLean, was something she refused to analyse too deeply. Jilly's teasing comment that she had all day to set about winning her bet did absolutely nothing for her equipoise and only added to her reluctance to have their outing get under way.

Kley's cruiser, *Sea Dancer*, was tied to the jetty ready for boarding, so evidently Kley was already on board. However, he was nowhere to be seen and Dave hailed him as he jumped lightly down into the back of the boat. There was a muffled voice from the inner workings of the craft and Dave's head disappeared for a moment and then reappeared.

'Pass your gear down, girls. Kley won't be long. He's making some very technical last-minute adjustments.'

'That sounds somewhat ominous,' remarked Jilly, descending the ladder first and stepping across into the boat with no trouble at all.

Brooke followed her a trifle nervously down the perpendicular steps and swung one foot gingerly on to the gently undulating deck. She moved to shift the rest of her body across just as the boat rocked sharply on a swell, overbalancing her into Dave's arms. He manfully took her weight and set her back on to her feet.

'Oh, Dave, I'm sorry. I haven't hurt you, have I?' she asked worriedly. 'I hope I'm not going to be too much of a landlubber.'

Dave laughed heartily. 'Not in the least, Brooke. Any time you want to throw yourself into my arms, feel free!'

She joined in his laughter and turned to step away so that Dave could stow the bags in their proper places. Her eyes encountered Kley's as he moved out from under the bimini top, wiping his hands on an oily rag. His face was set in an uncompromising expression and he barely acknowledged her tentative smile of greeting. Her stomach plummeted alarmingly as she recognised anger in the set of his jaw.

Jilly slipped into the breech once again. 'Hi, Kley! Everything ready to go?' she asked, unaware of the tension that set Brooke's teeth on edge.

'Sure is.' His voice sounded quite normal. 'My mate, Bill, keeps the boat in excellent condition when I'm not here to use her. I've just been adjusting a new cable he said he replaced last week.'

Dave had moved up to the bow ready to cast off the mooring rope as Kley turned and pressed the starter. The fifty h.p. outboard motor raced into life and the sixteen-foot cruiser edged out from the jetty and moved slowly towards the open bay.

Feeling the bite of the sun already, Brooke began applying protective lotion to the exposed surfaces of her arms and legs, not without some difficulty, as the breeze tended to blow her hair about her face, impairing her vision. Dave came to her assistance and gathered her hair in his hands, holding it back until she had finished. She smiled her thanks.

'Better not get too much sun, Brooke,' he advised her. 'Why don't you sit under the canopy with Kley?'

'How long will the trip across take?' Brooke asked, reluctant to make the first move towards Kley. After all, apart from his casual nod when she came aboard he hadn't spoken to her or, to her knowledge, looked in her direction, for that matter.

'Roughly twenty minutes, perhaps a bit longer, depending on the conditions,' Dave was saying. 'The island's eight kilometres or so from Townsville.'

Brooke considered the pros and cons of remaining on the open deck. They would no doubt be swimming later and walking on the beach in the sun, so if she didn't want a nasty dose of sunburn, she had better swallow her pride and take the seat in the shade beside Kley as Dave suggested. It was only for half an hour when all was said and done.

'Do you mind if I share some of your shade?' She

forced a smile into her voice as she slid into the seat by his side.

He glanced quickly at her and then turned his attention back to the boat, his large hands firmly on the steering wheel. 'Be my guest,' he said without expression, as Jilly came and stood between them, one slim hand resting lightly on Kley's shoulder and the other on the back of Brooke's seat to steady herself.

'There's nothing like the colour of that water, is there, Brooke?' she remarked.

Brooke murmured agreement, astounded at the way her heart twisted at the sight of Jilly's hand resting lightly on Kley's shoulder. She had never experienced such an intensity of feeling before in her life, a feeling that couldn't be jealousy. Surely she couldn't be jealous, not of Jilly and Kley MacLean? Even when Stephen had shown his preference for Samantha she hadn't felt any jealousy, only that devastating hurt and despair.

She pulled herself up short. She must be mad to be thinking this way about a man she had known for less than forty-eight hours, a man she had disliked intensely before she had even met him and who had not given her any reason since to change that opinion.

Surreptitiously she watched him out of the corner of her eye. He wore quite short black shorts and a white towelling shirt, laced at the front, and her eyes lingered on the play of his muscular thighs as he braced himself against the movement of the cruiser. There was latent power in every inch of his well-built body. Her own body began to burn as she realised the trend her thoughts were taking, and she almost started in fright as Jilly touched her arm and drew her attention to the approaching island.

'It's quite rugged, isn't it?' she said, gathering her scattered wits. Even from this distance the rocky peaks stood out boldly against the greenery of the island.

Kley turned towards her at the sound of her voice. 'The highest peak is that one over there, Mount Cook.

It rises some five hundred metres, and if you take a look at it through the binoculars,' he took them from the panel in front of him and passed them to her, 'you'll be able to see just how rugged it is. You might be able to pick out a few of the huge balancing granite boulders.'

'It's very densely wooded.' Brooke ran the binoculars over the island.

'They're mainly gums and hoop pines,' said Kley, 'with she-oaks, pandanus palms, and large banyan trees, which give the island different characteristics from those of the other tropical resorts of the Great Barrier Reef waters. The island's now a National Park and covers an area of roughly fifty-two square kilometres.'

'It was named Magnetic Island by Captain Cook in 1770, wasn't it?' asked Jilly. 'Didn't he think something in the stone of the island upset his compass or something?'

'Can't you tell she only teaches physical education?' remarked Dave.

'What do you mean "only" physical education?' exclaimed Jilly. 'Some of us look after their minds and some of us look after their bodies. It all fits together very nicely, for your information, Dave Martin!'

By now they were close by the island and Brooke could make out some activity in what Jilly told her was the main settlement of Picnic Bay. The colourful passenger ferry was moored to one side of the jetty and a few people were fishing from the other side into the blue-green water.

Kley changed the cruiser's direction slightly and soon they were passing Hawkins Point and made their way across Rocky, Nellee and Geoffrey Bays to the southern side of the island. Rounding Bremner Point, Kley throttled the engine back and gently idled into Alma Bay, nosing the boat towards a sturdy private jetty on the higher side of the bay.

Looking up from the jetty, Brooke shaded her eyes,

following a steepish path up the rocky hill to a house set about half way up. She could make out a woman's figure on the patio while a young boy bounded sure-footedly down the pathway.

Dave had gone to the bow again and jumped ashore as the cruiser gently nudged the rubber tyres tied to the jetty posts to act as buffers. Kley switched off the engine as Dave secured the bow rope and then caught the stern rope that Kley tossed him. When he had secured the cruiser Jilly passed up their bags to him and he held out his hand to Jilly to help her up the half metre or so on to the wooden decking. Kley steadied her with his hands on her hips until she was standing beside Dave.

In her eagerness to get on to the jetty without Kley's help, Brooke hurried forward, and in her haste tripped over a rubber mat on the deck of the boat. Kley's hands went instinctively out to her, preventing her from falling any further. His face registered cynical amusement at her alacrity to move away from him. By the time he had hoisted her on to firm ground again she was quite breathless, and she knew it wasn't caused by any physical exertion on her part. She watched the muscles of his legs flex and then he was beside them on the jetty.

'Hey, Kley! Kley! Hi there!' A dark-haired youth bounded down the last section of the pathway and on to the jetty, breathing deeply from his hasty descent from the house.

At closer quarters the lad looked older than Brooke had at first thought him to be. He was at that lanky stage where he seemed all arms and legs and he gave the impression that he was going to be every bit as tall as his uncle.

Stopping in front of them he put his hands on his hips, beaming at them all, one fine dark eyebrow rising when his gaze encountered Brooke. Dave and Jilly both knew him, and Dave turned to Brooke.

'Brooke, this is Kley's troublesome nephew, Drew.

And Drew, meet Brooke, a friend from Brisbane,' he said.

Brooke smiled at the boy and he half smiled back. She could feel he was weighing her up, then he turned his attention back to Kley and his grin widened.

'It's good to see you, Kley. How long are you staying?'

'Only for the day,' his uncle replied, putting his arm about the boy's shoulders as they started walking along the jetty. 'We're going back to Townsville this evening and I've arranged for Dave to collect you later in the week. He's staying in Townsville until Friday, so he'll bring you and Aunt Peg home.'

'Why can't you stay, too?' asked Drew, obviously disappointed with the arrangements. 'We expected you to stay a couple of days with us at least.'

'I have to get back to the station, you know that. I only came down to check up on the new four-wheel-drive we ordered last month. It should be ready by Friday, so Dave will drive you back in that.'

They started up the path to the house. To the right was a sturdy boat shed with two large doors and a grooved ramp, which meant that the cruiser must at some stage be winched up out of the water and into the shed. The cattle prices might fluctuate, but Kley Mac-Lean seemed to be reasonably well off, thought Brooke disparagingly.

Kley and Drew led the way up the hill with Dave following, complaining about the weight of the girls' bags. Jilly dropped back to walk alongside Brooke.

'What do you think of the island so far?' she asked. 'Beautiful, isn't it?'

Brooke nodded. 'The water's just beckoning me in for a swim.' She turned her head for another look at the crystal clear waters of the bay and promptly tripped over a rock in the pathway. This put the two girls a few paces behind the others. She mentally chastised herself for her clumsiness, first on the boat and now on the path. Since the advent of Kley MacLean into her life she seemed to be right out of her orbit. She watched his dark head disappear around a bend in the pathway.

'How old is—er—Kley's nephew?' she asked Jilly, hesitating over saying his name.

'Drew? Let's see, about thirteen, I think. He's tall for his age, isn't he? Actually he looks very much like Kley, but Drew's a lot darker complexioned, which I think he gets from his father. He had quite dark olive skin. Drew's mother was Kley's sister. Fiona was a year or so younger than Kley and after their father died she eloped with some ne'er-do-well fellow. They came back to work on the Downs when Drew was a baby but, unfortunately, Fiona died giving birth to her stillborn second child. Her husband left Drew in Kley's care when he pushed off to supposedly greener pastures. So Kley has virtually raised him.'

'That's quite a responsibility,' said Brooke.

'Yes. Aunt Connie was telling me they've had a bit of trouble with him this year and he was pretty well expelled from one school. Oh, he's bright enough, a bit too bright, if you ask me, and. . . .'

'Come on, you two slowcoaches, shake a leg!' called Dave, and the subject of Kley's nephew was closed.

The MacLean house was quite new and built into the hillside, with crossed steel beams and supports. It seemed that their old house had been badly damaged in Cyclone Althea and Kley had decided to demolish it and erect a new cyclone-proof building. The house consisted of one main living floor with a wide covered deck overlooking the bay while the underneath was used as a garage, laundry and storeroom. A bright yellow Minimoke, not in its first bloom of youth, a small motorcycle, probably a trail bike, and a pushbike were parked in the garage.

After she had been made known to Aunt Peg, a pleasant-faced middle-aged woman with whom Dave was going to board in the Towers, Jilly showed her the rest of the house. It was a true tropical holiday house, designed to let in as much air as possible. There were three bedrooms, a bathroom, kitchen and dining area, as well as the largest open living room Brooke had seen.

A short time later they walked down to the sandy beach for a swim before lunch. Drew carried a large colourful beach umbrella and they set off down another branch of the pathway between granite boulders of various sizes and they were soon down on the hot white sand of the beach where they were to swim.

Brooke was glad that by the time she had removed her shorts and top and had folded them carefully beside her beach towel, Kley was swimming out from the shore with Dave and Drew.

'Race you in!' called Jilly, her face alive with mischief, and Brooke shed her self-consciousness and plunged into the cool water with the other girl, letting herself luxuriate in the pleasure of the cool salty water on her hot body.

Dave was the first to rejoin the girls, swimming underneath the water and spearing up to duck Jilly, who spluttered to the surface and chased after him, bent upon revenge. When Kley and Drew returned to the shallower water they joined in the game of water chase, and Brooke was soon out of breath.

She was a relatively strong swimmer and managed to evade Dave and Jilly, but her limbs turned to jelly when Kley's strong brown arms struck out, propelling himself in her direction, overtaking her in a dozen strokes. Firm muscular arms, gleaming wetly in the sunlight, folded around her waist from behind.

'You didn't put up much of a fight to get away, Brooke,' laughed Dave from some distance away, shaking his wet hair from his eyes.

'Did you try to get away or did you let me catch you, Brooke?' asked a deep mellow voice somewhere near her right ear.

His breath moving faintly against her sensitive earlobe had Brooke gulping in air as though she had almost drowned, when in actual fact her head was a good half metre above the waves. The feel of his smooth firm body against her back made her feel light-headed and reckless. She turned her head slightly.

'Would I do that?' she asked teasingly. 'You were just simply too fast for me, Mr MacLean.' Her eyelashes fell demurely beneath his gaze.

He looked at her for a moment and then grinned. 'I do believe you're flirting with me, Miss Drynan, and that can be very dangerous. Very dangerous indeed.' His hands moved caressingly against her waist and then she found herself being lifted and dumped unceremoniously into the waves.

When she surfaced, gasping and brushing her hair back from her face, he was treading water a couple of metres away. His teeth flashed white against his tanned face as his grin challenged her.

She set off determinedly, but was no match for him in speed. However, she did manage to outmanoeuvre Drew and then it was his turn to give chase. It didn't take long for the strenuous game to tire them and they returned to the beach, thankfully resting on the sand while their swimsuits dried in the sun.

For Brooke, those moments sitting in the hot shade of the beach umbrella were a form of pleasurable torment. She found her eyes straying back to Kley's brown body as he lay on his stomach with his face on his arms, inviting the sun's tanning of his already bronzed back. When he shifted slightly his muscles rippled in the brightness and she had to resolutely push aside the desire to reach out and touch the firm flesh of his shoulders and run her fingers lingeringly down his spine.

'You'll probably fall for him.' Jilly's words came back to her. Never! she told herself firmly, turning her eyes back to the beauty of the water rippling on to the sand. If she did watch him it was purely in an aesthetic manner, much as you would admire a good painting or an interesting piece of sculpture. Her eyes were drawn back again as he shifted into a more comfortable position, and suddenly her pulses raced. She was shocked and dismayed at the intensity of feeling this man who was virtually a stranger evoked within her.

In all the years she had known Stephen she couldn't remember ever once feeling such a depth of response to his nearness. Maybe that was what had been missing from their relationship. At least this half hour had proved one thing to her. When Stephen had left she had had to fight down the tiny spark of insecurity which had threatened to flame into mammoth proportions, that she had been to blame for their break-up, that she had failed him in some way. It had crossed her tormented mind that perhaps she was frigid and unable to share any kind of physical relationship with anyone, but one glance at Kley MacLean soon tore that theory to shreds.

It was purely physical attraction, she assured herself. She would feel the same about any reasonably attractive man, especially now that she was beginning to shed the emotional burden that Stephen's rejection had heaped upon her. She must try to remember that she was all at once susceptible.

But Dave Martin is a reasonably attractive man, said a small voice inside her, and you don't get all flustered over him. She wasn't getting flustered, she told herself, her eyes once more on that brown body, impressing on herself that she disliked everything Kley MacLean's attitude stood for. At that precise moment her senses didn't seem to be taking the slightest bit of notice.

Then she found herself wondering what it would be like to be held in his arms, have his lips touch hers, his hands caress her. Her body burned and she hastily pulled her thoughts into order. But that didn't stop her eyes from being drawn persistently back to the figure on the sand, like a moth drawn to a flame.

Feeling secure in the anonymity of her dark-lensed

sunglasses, Brooke gave in to her thoughts and just allowed her eyes to rove all over his still form. Suddenly he turned over on to his back, dusting the sand from his legs and chest and then settling back with his arms folded across his forehead to shield his eyes from the sun. Quickly she looked away, and although she knew he couldn't possibly have seen her eyes on him, she was sure he was aware of her regard and that he was neither amused nor impressed by her attention.

'What's the hold-up with the new four-wheel-drive, Kley?' asked Drew, idly picking up handfuls of white sand and letting it filter slowly through his fingers.

'Nothing much. I've had them add a carrier to the top to hold the water containers we need when we spend some time away working on the fences, and an extra bit of tubing on the bull bars up front. I think that's about it. If we get half the work out of the new one that we did out of the old one, I'll be happy,' replied his uncle sleepily.

'How are you getting back to the Downs, then, if you're leaving the old bus in Townsville?' enquired Drew.

'I'll probably take the train in the morning. We left the ute at Aunt Peg's, so I can get back home from the Towers all right. I'm not looking forward to the long slog at the mercy of the railways, though,' he grimaced.

'No worries, Kley. You can go with Brooke and Jilly,' said Dave. 'They're leaving for the Towers in the morning and they won't mind taking you along. They'd probably welcome the company, if you can stand Jilly's incessant chatter, that is. If you're lucky she'll go to sleep.'

'I resent that remark, Dave Martin,' Jilly murmured, piling a handful of sand in the middle of his bare chest.

At Dave's offer a flicker of dismay had passed across Brooke's face before she could school her features, and it had not gone unnoticed, if the tightening of Kley's mouth was anything to go by. He had raised himself into a sitting position with one effortless movement and looked coldly at her.

'You're going to the Towers tomorrow?' he asked evenly.

Brooke nodded a little selfconsciously, quivering inwardly with a mixture of feelings. The thought of a hundred and thirty-five kilometres of Kley's company next day caused her to feel quite exhilarated and, at the same time, apprehensive, as though a little voice warned her she must be wary. But of course Jilly would be going too, she reminded herself, breathing a little easier.

'I'd appreciate a lift, if that's acceptable to you?' the last part was only slightly sarcastic, 'then I could be back at work by lunch time instead of losing another day.'

'Of ... of course,' stammered Brooke. 'It's fine with me.'

'Me, too,' Jilly beamed at Kley.

'That's nicely settled, then,' said Dave. 'How about lunch? All this strenuous activity has given me a mountainous appetite!'

Lunch was a jovial affair with the whole party making short work of the fresh salads and tropical fruit that Aunt Peg had set out on a large folding table on the patio deck. Brooke especially enjoyed the fresh fruit salad which Aunt Peg had made herself from diced pawpaw, pineapple, bananas, passionfruit, kiwi fruit and orange and lemon juices, and topped with soft whipped cream.

'There'll be no snorkelling for us for ages, that's for sure,' sighed Dave, leaning back in his chair, replete. 'We'd go straight to the bottom like sacks of rocks.'

'Perhaps Brooke would like a tour of the island in the car for an hour or so,' suggested Aunt Peg.

'I'd be as happy reclining here in the shade, just me and my lunch,' laughed Dave, patting his stomach.

'The moke will only take four, five at a pinch,' remarked Drew.

'If Brooke doesn't mind, I'll stay here with Dave,' said Jilly, 'and help Aunt Peg clear lunch away.' She gave Brooke a conspiratorial wink behind Kley's back.

'Well, so far, there's the driver,' said Kley, 'I guess that's me, and Brooke. Want to come along, Drew?'

Much to Jilly's disgust Drew elected to accompany them.

Walking down to the car, Brooke felt an inner thankfulness for Drew's presence. She really couldn't see why everyone thought he was troublesome when she had decided he was a friend for life. And besides, it would be a brief respite to escape Jilly's winks and eyebrow-raising innuendoes for a while, even if she did have to share a car with Kley MacLean. It would be practice for tomorrow, she grinned to herself.

As they bumped along in the little open car, Drew overcame some of his earlier reserve with Brooke and, more often than not, it was the young boy rather than Kley who pointed out to her the various places of interest. They drove around to Horseshoe Bay, past the Koala Park, and a couple of times Kley brought the car to a halt in the laybys so that Brooke could get out for a better look. From the road the views of the clear water and the reef below were magnificent.

While at Picnic Bay, the most populated part of the island, the three of them walked the length of the jetty, stopping here and there to ask if the hopeful fishermen had had any luck. When they returned to the car Drew decided he wanted an ice cream, and when Kley and Brooke declined his offer to get them one as well, he loped off to a small shop, leaving Brooke and Kley alone for the moment.

Brooke felt a sudden tension between them and was searching for a non-committal topic of conversation when Kley broke the uncomfortable silence that had fallen with Drew's departure.

'What time did you intend leaving for the Towers in the morning?' he asked, his gaze following a couple of seagulls over the water.

'Any time,' she replied. 'I mean, we haven't decided on any set time. I shall just have to telephone our land-lady before we leave to let her know we'll be arriving at last. We were due to arrive there last Friday.'

'What do you plan on doing in the Towers?' he asked. 'Will you be staying long?'

'Do?' Brooke looked at him blankly. 'What do you mean?'

'As far as a job's concerned.'

'Oh, a job,' she smiled. 'I'm a teacher—I thought Dave told you. I've been transferred to the same school as Dave and Jilly. At the High School.'

A number of expressions crossed his face. 'I wouldn't have picked you as a teacher,' he said at last, his tone giving her the impression that he didn't think she was capable of holding down any job, let alone that one. His eyes met hers mockingly. 'They didn't make teach-ers like you in my day.'

'I'm surprised they had teachers in your day,' she replied sweetly.

His head rose and he looked down his arrogant nose. 'You have a sharp tongue, Brooke. I hope you're as sharp in the classroom.'

Brooke raised her eyebrows enquiringly as Drew ap-proached, tackling his ice cream with gusto, intent upon saving the sticky drops from falling before he could lick them up.

'They've had four teachers from the High School this year that I know of who have thrown in the towel and resigned or demanded transfers, so I don't like your chances of making a go of it,' he stated, climbing back behind the steering wheel of the Mini-moke as Drew joined them.

CHAPTER FOUR

'LET'S see if this mask is a tight fit.' Kley handed Brooke a diving mask from the box of snorkelling gear. 'Put it completely against your face and breathe in gently. If the mask stays on without the head strap to hold it in place then it's the right fit.'

The second one Brooke tried fitted perfectly. She controlled her features not to flinch away from his touch or allow him to see that she still seethed from his earlier remarks. He had a colossal nerve! There was no way he could possibly gauge her capabilities as a teacher, but he was prepared to reject her ability out of hand.

That bet of Jilly's, the temptation to put her outrageous plan into action, was great at this moment. How she'd love to see him taken down a peg or two! She looked at him through her lashes as he reached for his own mask to demonstrate the techniques. Dared she? Why not? asked a devilish voice inside her. She would have to take care, though. She had a feeling if she muffed it, she could get burned.

'Now,' Kley continued, 'if you seal the mask over your face before you pull the strap around the back of your head then you won't pull your hair down into the mask to interfere with the seal. You see, if the mask gets flooded then that defeats its purpose, which is to trap air over your eyes and give you clear vision in the water.'

They were in a large grey and orange inflatable dinghy. It had been taken for granted right from the outset that Kley would show Brooke the rudiments of the sport and Brooke would have liked to tell him just where she'd have liked him to go, but with her plans to

thwart him taking shape again she simply smiled and
submitted to his instructions. Whether or not he saw
through her sickly sweetness she didn't know, but the
close confines of the dinghy and his well-built and vir-
ilely attractive body were just too close to Brooke for
comfort and she had a sneaky feeling that the upper
hand in the situation could very easily be shifted to his
side of the boat.

Jilly had remained with Aunt Peg and Dave and
Drew had somersaulted overboard and were swimming
under the surface some way from the dinghy. When
Brooke questioned the way the other two had entered
the water, looking at Kley with large eyes, he had explained that to dive in head first would cause your mask
and snorkel to be slammed back into your face. The
best method of entry was to sit on the edge of the
dinghy, tuck your head into your chest, hold your mask
and snorkel in place and fall backwards so that you hit
the water with your shoulder blades.

'This J-shaped tube,' he was saying, 'is your snorkel
and it enables you to breathe while your head is under
water. You put the bite-piece between your teeth,' he
demonstrated, 'and this large oval flange surrounding
the bite-piece fits between your teeth and the inside of
your lips. When you purse your lips around it, it forms
a seal. You don't need to bite hard. Here, have a try.
Keep the tube of your snorkel on the left hand side of
your head. We'll have a practice in the water in a
moment.'

He reached around for the fins and chose the smallest
pair in the box, explaining that the longer and stiffer the
blades the more inclined she would be to getting muscle
cramps, not being used to the flippers. He helped her
buckle the fins on to her feet, his strong arm brushing
her shoulder and sparking the flame of tension between
them that always seemed to run close to the suface. He
gave no sign that he was aware of the change in the
atmosphere between them as he turned to buckle his

own flippers, but she noticed a pulse beating in the tightness of his square jaw. It was the first time she had been given any indication that he was in any way moved by her nearness, and it would have been a heady thought if her pulses weren't racing madly along with his.

'Right. Ready for a try-out?' he said flatly.

They slid over the side of the dinghy and he held her up with one arm around her waist and one over the side of the dinghy while she adjusted her mask, her heart beating loudly in her ears.

'How's it going?' Drew's head popped up beside them.

'Just about ready to give it a go,' replied his uncle, 'so leave us room to work. On second thoughts, you can hang on to Brooke while I show her how to work the snorkel in the water.'

Drew surged over, splashing Brooke and making her splutter. His young arm wrapped around her and he grinned cheekily from ear to ear. She gave him an uncertain smile and gingerly put her arm around his shoulders.

He laughed unselfconsciously. 'Something tells me you don't trust me, Brooke.' He looked uncannily like his uncle.

'Just be forewarned that I can swim and won't drown if you do let me go,' she laughed back.

'Heck, I wouldn't let you go,' he looked mortally wounded. 'Besides, it'll make Dave jealous if he sees us, won't it?'

Before Brooke could comment his uncle broke in sharply. 'If you're going to be more of a hindrance than a help, Drew, you can go back to Dave.' His brows were drawn together in an irritated frown. 'Now, let's practice breathing through the snorkel, Brooke. Got it sealed in place? Put your face under the water and breathe slowly through your mouth. Once you get the hang of it, it's easy.'

Once she felt she had mastered breathing through the snorkel confidently Kley moved her on to clearing the snorkel if she wanted to go deeper and submerged its opening.

'Just take a breath before you go under, and don't worry about plugging the end of the snorkel with your tongue because no water will come into your mouth unless you suck it in. You needn't even lift your face out of the water to clear the tube, just give a simple puff and it will clear. Okay, have a try.'

A short time later she was ready to go. 'Drew and I will be on either side of you. Just remember to swing your legs from your hips and not the knee, okay? Mask and snorkel feel comfortable?'

Brooke nodded and they moved away from the dinghy. An exciting new world opened up below her. They swam above the seabed of swaying plantlife and watched the fish of various colours and sizes flit about their domain. Dave joined them and motioned them to follow him to a more colourful section of the seabed. By the time they climbed back into the dinghy Brooke was physically exhausted but ecstatic over her new adventure.

'I was going to suggest we go around for a walk on the reef,' said Dave, 'but I think it might be a bit much for one day for Brooke, don't you, Kley?'

'Yes, her muscles are going to protest tomorrow as it is, so I think you should take it easy for the rest of the day,' said Kley.

They all sat down. The king had spoken, it seemed.

'Anyone want to come for a walk around the headland?' asked Drew, who had revitalised himself after three-quarters of an hour of relaxation on the patio. No one seemed enthusiastic.

'How far did you plan on walking?' asked Brooke, taking pity at Drew's disappointed expression.

'Oh, it's a fair hike. Around that rocky outcrop,' he pointed across the bay. 'On the other side there's lots of interesting marine creatures in the rock pools.'

Brooke looked doubtful.

'Oh, come on, Brooke. I'll double you on the bike,' he pleaded.

'The one downstairs?' Brooke began.

'I hope you haven't been riding the motorbike on the road again, Drew,' Kley interrupted sternly.

'Course not, Kley. I was only joking. You know I'm not old enough to get my licence,' he replied. 'I meant my pushbike.'

'Well, I could double you on the motorcycle,' said Brooke. 'I've got my motorcycle licence.'

'What a bag of surprises the girl is!' remarked Dave. 'She's a bikie to boot.'

'Hardly that, Dave. My brothers belong to a bike club and sometimes they let me ride their bikes, in motorcross and hill climbs. Really, I'm quite capable.' She dug into her bag for her licence and showed it to Drew's uncle.

He glanced at it and handed it back, making no comment.

'Great,' beamed Drew. 'We've got two helmets downstairs. I'll dig them out.'

'Are you sure it's all right?' she asked in Kley's direction, regretting her impulsiveness.

'If you want to go,' was all he said, but he followed them downstairs and watched while she kicked the engine over.

It went on the third try and, strapping her helmet in place, she nodded to Drew to climb aboard.

He arranged himself comfortably on the back and wrapped his arms around her waist, grinning broadly. 'Don't wait up for us, Unc.'

'Don't stay too long. I'd like to get back to Townsville before dark,' Kley remarked loudly as Brooke idled the bike out of the garage.

She raised her hand in acknowledgement as she pulled away from the house. They followed the road around the bay and veered along a rough track that Drew pointed out. The bike lurched over the ruts and stones until they reached a small clear area where Drew indicated they leave the motorbike.

Brooke switched off the engine and, removing her skid-lid and setting it on the seat, she took a towelling hat out of her pocket and plonked it on her head. She followed Drew between two boulders and they were looking down on a rocky beach. It was strewn with boulders of various sizes and shapes, weathered smooth. They started down an easy incline to the beach.

'See those little groups of molluscs there?' Drew pointed out and Brooke nodded. 'Well, they're called melaraphe and they feed on the spray. This section is the supra-littoral zone, which is never covered by the tide.'

'Periwinkles,' Brooke bent down for a closer inspection of the little shells, some plain, others patterned. 'This must be the littoral zone, right?'

Drew looked at her closely. 'Do you know all about the zones, too?'

'I've read a bit about it and I studied some zoology in college, but I've probably forgotten more than I remember,' she laughed, 'so feel free to jog my memory.'

She had a feeling that all this was a favourite subject of Kley's nephew.

'Well, let's see.' He warmed to his subject. 'This is the littoral zone and it's divided into three parts, upper, mid and lower. Very logical,' he grinned. 'Many of the animals in these areas require very fixed conditions to exist, but others can take more variations.

'The upper section is also called the barnacle zone,' he pointed some out on the rocks nearby, 'because of the predominance of barnacles. Also logical. Although barnacles are shellfish-like in appearance, they're actually crustaceans and feed on the plankton in the sea spray.'

They moved further down the beach.

'The oysters start here. That's basically the beginning of the mid-littoral zone. You can practically see the dividing line between the two sections.' He produced a sturdy penknife from his pocket and dexterously removed an oyster from its shell in a rock pool and popped it in his mouth. 'Want one?'

'No, thanks,' Brooke screwed up her nose. 'I can't stand the thought of them sliding down.'

He laughed and swallowed a few more, then he motioned her closer. 'See these little knobby shells,' he pointed to a blackish shell about three-quarters of an inch long and covered all over with whitish bumps, 'they're oyster borers and they feed on the oysters. This one here is a chiton. They wedge between the oysters and even in old oyster cases.'

They found chitons up to two and a half inches in length and, when touched, they secreted a glue-like substance which served as a type of cement to prevent their removal from the rocks. More numerous than the chitons were the limpets, some smooth, others corrugated. Small crabs, barely a quarter of an inch across, skittered here and there when the beachcombers drew near. Their colours were various, with orange-brown being the most common, all blending with the rock and sand backdrop of their habitat.

Close by the water's edge they found tent shells, grey in colour with a pink spotted longitudinal pattern, the animals crawling along the surface of their substratum with the aid of an extended muscular foot which could be withdrawn into the shell opening. This opening was then covered by the operculum, or lid, an ochre-coloured protective device.

Drew pointed out a number of deadly cone shells, two of which had been claimed by hermit crabs and one very attractive specimen patterned in black and orange checks which was very much alive.

'These shells are some of the most sought after of the gastropods, but you have to be very careful handling them,' he told her as he used a piece of stick to discover that a beige-coloured cone shell was now uninhabited.

'Do you know, Brooke, that these cone shells have been
known to sting through a leather glove? The radula
consists of a series of dart-like teeth arranged in pairs in
the radula sac, which are carried forward one at a time
into the proboscis, a sort of suctorial organ. Poison is
secreted into the hollow teeth which have complexly
barbed tips. The proboscis comes out from the narrow
end of the shell and can bend around towards the rear,
so that's why you have to handle them warily. Some of
the cones feed on fish, some on molluscs and some on
worms.' Brooke was impressed again by the boy's
knowledge of the marine life and when she remarked on
this he grinned, obviously well pleased.

'Kley gave me a couple of great books on marine life
and shells because he knows I'd like to take up marine
biology eventually. I've got a fairly big collection of
shells at home on the Downs and I really enjoy identify-
ing the specimens. I've even exchanged shells with
people overseas. Maybe I could show them to you some
time?'

'I'd be interested to see them,' said Brooke, bending
down to gently turn over a rock in a shallow pool.
Under the rock were some red waratah anemones, re-
sembling red cherries as they closed their tentacles as
Brooke lifted the rock out of the water. A bright green
anemone at the very bottom of the rock had tiny pieces
of sand and shell in its tentacles, and when Drew
touched it with his piece of stick, it withdrew its tentacles, the sand and shell serving as camouflage. Brooke
just as carefully replaced the rock. They uncovered lots
more of the little polyps as they browsed along the
water's edge.

Moving towards a group of rock pools, Drew caught
a glimpse of movement in the shadow of a submerged
rock. This proved to be a sea hare, and the boy was
most excited as it was the first one he had seen this
holiday. The elusive creature was mottled brown,
almost leopardskin, in colour and had two extended

feelers. Holding it up for examination, Drew gently folded back the skin to show Brooke the black shell beneath, which bore a regular line of holes along one edge. The underside was a light olive green and muscular.

'This is great fun, isn't it?' Drew looked up at Brooke, and she was reminded once more of his resemblance to his uncle. 'I really enjoy fossicking around. Let's turn up a few more rocks. We should uncover some sea cucumbers.'

They walked along the seashore in companionable enjoyment, stopping here and there to examine some small discovery. One rock yielded a brittle star, its roughly pentagonal-shaped body decorated on the dorsal side with a black flower-like pattern while the ventral side bore an ochre star-like design. The five appendages, like spindly legs, had their own black and grey coloured camouflage. Drew uncovered some of his sea cucumbers, tube-footed creatures, reminiscent of a bloated sausage, which ejected a white, rubbery substance when provoked.

They came upon a colony of soft coral, above and below the water line. Underwater, with its tentacles waving, it was an attractive green, while out of the water it was a drab grey, its tentacles closed to prevent desiccation.

Drew called from a crevice between the short rock face and a large boulder. They were working their way back to where they had left the bike and in the quiet shady pool at the base of the crevice Drew showed her what resembled a flowering anemone. When he passed his hand over the creature it withdrew down a tube cemented to the rock. As they watched it slowly re-emerged, gradually extending its tentacles.

'What do you suppose it is, Brooke? I can't say I've even noticed anything like that before,' he frowned.

'Could be a fan worm, polychaete, I think they're called,' she replied. 'You'll have to look it up in your books when you get home.'

'How do you spell polychaete?' he asked, proceeding
to sketch the fan worm in a small notebook he dug out
of the pocket of his shorts.

Brooke watched his face as he concentrated on sketch-
ing in as much detail as possible. Although his skin was
quite olive brown and his eyes and hair were jet black,
the line of his jaw and the full curve of his lips promised
to be as rugged and attractive as his uncle's, and he
would surely be as tall as Kley. No doubt in a few years
he would be breaking as many hearts, she thought drily.

She wondered about his mother—Fiona, Jilly said
her name had been. Tragically her life had been short
and she had missed the emergence of her son from
babyhood to youthful adolescence. She sighed and
Drew looked up and caught her eyes on him. He
flashed her an unselfconscious grin.

'You look a lot like your uncle,' she spoke her
thoughts, feeling somewhat embarrassed to be caught
watching him so intently.

He chuckled in his almost deep voice. 'So everyone
tells me. Good-looking lot, aren't we?' he asked outrageously. 'My mother looked a lot like Kley, too—at
least she does in the photos I've seen of her. I guess I
can't exactly bring her face to mind. She died when I
was about three or four years old.' He had sobered, his
youthful face, with its promise of rugged manhood,
suddenly young and vulnerable. 'But I kind of remember having her there, though. She used to sing to
me.' He shrugged his shoulders as though he thought he
had said too much. 'I've lived with Kley ever since. And
Dougal, of course.'

'Dougal?' she asked. 'Who's Dougal?'

Drew grinned again. 'You could say he's our house-
keeper, if you're very brave.' He chuckled at his own
joke. 'He's a distant relative of the family. He came out
from Scotland to work on the Downs when he was

about my age and he's been there ever since. He injured his leg pretty badly ages ago when he was thrown from a horse he was breaking, so now he does all the chores in the house. He's a pretty good cook—if you're not too fussy about Cordon Bleu, that is,' he laughed. 'He makes a mean apple pie. Mmmm! He's Aunt Peg's father.'

'Oh,' said Brooke. 'I thought Aunt Peg was your uncle's aunt.'

'Let's not get too complicated now,' he teased. 'No, Aunt Peg's not really our aunt. She's a widow and she lives in this huge old house in the Towers. I board with her during the week and we all stay with her when we come into town from Terebori Downs. Dave will be staying there, too.

'Dave's a nice guy. Everyone likes him.' He looked at her for a moment. 'Is he your boy-friend?'

Brooke laughed at his serious expression. 'No. Dave and I are just good friends, that's all.'

Drew regarded her a little sceptically. 'On the level?'

She nodded, her eyes twinkling. 'On the level.'

'Oh,' he said, 'I just wondered. I know he's married to Jacqui, but I thought you might have been his new bird. He said you were a friend of his and I thought he meant girl-friend.'

'No. Just friends.'

'Does that mean you're kind of free and unattached?' he asked.

'If you mean do I have a steady boy-friend, then yes, I'm free and unattached,' she replied amusedly.

He shook his head. 'What's wrong with the guys down in Brisbane? How come they let a spunky bird like you get away from them?'

'I guess I was just lucky,' she laughed.

'I don't have a regular girl-friend either,' he said seriously. 'Kley and I are going to stay bachelors.'

Brooke raised her eyebrows. 'Are you just?'

'Yes. Kley says women are life's biggest complications, especially now they want to run everything, and he says he has enough on his plate without adding liberated women to it. Are you a liberated woman, Brooke?' he asked with a grin.

'Very liberated,' she replied emphatically, 'especially the way your uncle means.'

'Pity,' remarked Drew. 'If Kley did want to get married I reckon he should pick someone like you.'

'Thanks for the compliment, but I'm not ready to get married at this particular time,' Brooke told him, imagining the look on his uncle's face had he heard him. 'I think we'd better be getting back now.'

They began walking up the path to the bike. 'This is your first trip up north, isn't it?' asked Drew, taking her hand to help her over a large rock. She murmured an affirmative. 'Did Dave take you to the top of Castle Hill?'

'He sure did,' she replied, catching her breath for a moment. 'We went up there on our comprehensive tour of the city yesterday morning.' Had it only been yesterday? 'And I'm looking forward to seeing Charters Towers, too. Terebori Downs is about fifty kilometres from the town, isn't it?' she asked him as they reached the clearing.

'Mmmm. Roughly north-west. The road out there isn't too bad when it's dry, and that's most of the time.' He pulled a face. 'It doesn't rain all that much out there, but when it does it chucks down buckets for a short time and then stops just as suddenly. The homestead's on a bit of a hill and there's a spring-fed creek we can swim in, so it's not so bad.'

'And you run cattle?' She felt as though she was pumping him for information—purely for conversational interest, she told herself.

Drew nodded. 'Mainly cattle and some horses. Kley wants to start breeding his own horses, but he hasn't had the time, what with one thing and another. Either the cattle prices drop or there's a drought on top of the drought, so he has to pretty well keep at it all the time to make ends meet. At least, that's what he tells me. But his ultimate aim is to have his own bloodstock, and keep the cattle, too, of course. Terebori Downs has always run cattle.'

There was a measure of family pride in his voice. 'You should see Kley's horse,' Drew's eyes were alight. 'He's really something. Kley says I can have my pick of his first colts.'

At that moment they both became aware of the sound of an engine coming slowly along the rutted track. Brooke glanced at Drew and he shrugged his shoulders, turning in the direction of the sound. They hadn't long to wait. The yellow Mini-moke rounded the corner with Kley at the wheel, his dark glasses flashing in the sun's flare.

'We were just about to head back,' said Drew as his uncle climbed agilely out of the little car. 'Did you think we'd got lost or something?'

'I came to hurry you along as I want to head off in about twenty minutes.' His gaze turned to Brooke. 'I had an idea Drew might try to coerce you into roaring from one end of the island to the other on the motor-cycle.'

He didn't wait for a comment, although Drew gave him a look of exaggeratedly wounded feelings.

'We'll put the bike on the back and I'll drive you home.' He took the bike from Brooke's hands and wheeled it around to the rear of the moke. Drew hurriedly grabbed one end of the machine and they lifted it and set the wheels in between two grooved pieces of steel that had been welded in place of the bumper bar section. Kley made a couple more adjustments at the top of the bike and then motioned Brooke into the front as Drew sprang into the back.

Well, really! He was the most high-handed man she had had the misfortune to meet, thought Brooke, as she subsided coolly into the seat. He hadn't even asked if she preferred to drive back in the car, instead of riding the bike. He just gave the orders and everyone had to jump.

'Rats! I was rather looking forward to the ride back on the bike,' Drew voiced her feelings. 'You really needn't have come for us, Kley.'

'I didn't want to be manoeuvring *Sea Dancer* about in the dark,' was all Kley said as he expertly turned the Mini in the small clearing.

Brooke's eyes watched his strong hands as they manipulated the steering wheel, letting it slide through his fingers with a minimum of effort. And then she had to brace herself as they rocked over the excuse for a track. Brooke suspected he took some delight in causing as much discomfort as he could, and she was thankful when they turned on to the sealed road and headed back to the house.

'Dave will be back to pick you up later in the week, Drew,' said Kley as the young boy prepared to cast them off. 'I'll see you when you return to the Towers. Okay?' Kley raised his voice above the throb of the engine.

'Sure, Kley,' Drew yelled back. 'Say hi to Dougal for me and tell him I'm looking forward to some of his apple pie to boost me up ready for school on Monday.'

Kley waved and the cruiser edged out from the jetty. The wind had whipped up the sea and the sun had almost disappeared by the time they set foot on the jetty back in Townsville, and Brooke was more than happy to be on terra firma again, deciding she would never make a rough weather sailor.

Eyeing her pale face, Kley raised an amused eyebrow. 'Feeling queasy?'

'I'm fine,' she forced a smile, reluctant to have him think she was a namby-pamby. She took a deep breath of the clear salty air and pulled her jacket more closely around her shoulders.

'How about coming back for coffee and a snack, Kley?' asked Dave.

'Oh, I think I'll call it a day,' began his friend.

'Rubbish. You haven't anything on tonight, have you?' pressured Dave, and Kley shook his head. 'Well then, come on back with us.'

And so Kley's hired car followed them back up the hill to Dave's house. The verandah light burned brightly and as they climbed stiffly out of the car a slight figure followed by the plump form of Dave's mother came quickly down the steps to greet them.

At much the same moment Brooke noticed the concerned frown on Mrs Martin's face and heard Jilly's indrawn breath.

'What a something nerve!' muttered Jilly.

Brooke's eyes moved back to the young woman. She was tall and slim and her neat slacks and top were simple and flattered her figure. Her dark hair was pulled back into a chignon and she gave the appearance of being a very self-assured young woman.

Her flight down the stairs slowed only fractionally as Dave walked around the front of the car. His face was set and almost expressionless, although he had paled beneath the artificial light.

'Hello, Dave. It's nice to see you again.' Her voice was low and attractive and matched her controlled aura of self-possession.

'Hello, Jacqui,' replied Dave, his voice not giving away any of his feelings.

'I heard you were back, Dave, so I thought I'd drop in to see you.' She turned and her eyes took in the two girls. 'Hello, Jilly. How are you?'

'Not bad,' Jilly replied, obviously reluctant to talk to the girl.

Jacqui's gaze turned curiously on Brooke and then Dave was beside her, his arm around Brooke's waist as he drew her closer. 'Jacqui, this is Brooke,' his fingers tightened on her waist, 'a friend from Brisbane. Brooke, meet Jacqui.'

'Hello, Jacqui.' Brooke could feel her face flame with embarrassment as she tried to move away from Dave, but he held her fast.

Not by as much as a flicker of her eyelids did the other girl betray any upset as her eyes took in Dave's hand on Brooke's waist. Then her eyes moved past them and she smiled eagerly and stepped towards Kley as he joined them. 'Kley! Good to see you again.' Her arms went around him for a moment as she lifted her cheek for his kiss, and then she stepped back. 'Dave's mother mentioned you were in town.'

'Jacqui—beautiful as ever.' Kley's eyes smiled down at the other girl, causing a small pang somewhere in the pit of Brooke's stomach. However, when his eyes moved over Brooke and Dave as they stood together the smile died and his look froze into shafts of steel.

'Well, come on into the house and I'll make us all a nice cup of tea,' Dave's mother broke the stiff silence that had fallen, and they all moved quietly upstairs.

The half hour or so that followed was the most uncomfortable Brooke had experienced. Jilly, usually most talkative and volatile, was quiet and morose, while Dave, sitting close to Brooke and favouring her every so often with a nice smile, was at his most eloquent, exuding a general bonhomie and 'all's right with the world'.

When Kley spoke his voice was even and controlled, while his eyes, which only moved to Brooke when he couldn't possibly avoid looking at her, were deep and glacial.

Well, Jilly Martin, thought Brooke a little hysterically, at this moment your dollar is as safe as the Bank of England!

Eventually Jacqui decided it was time to leave and Kley kindly offered to drop her home to save her calling a taxi. As the car pulled away everyone seemed to breathe a sigh of relief, although no one made any comment on Jacqui's visit.

'I hope you and Jilly like the flat that's being saved for you,' said Mrs Martin later as they relaxed on the verandah in the cool breeze.

'I'm sure we will,' replied Brooke. 'It sounds quite compact and it's only one street away from the school, so that's most convenient.'

'And Aunt Peg's house is only three or four blocks away as well, so I'll be nearby if you get lonesome,' Dave grinned.

'If you do get lonely, Brooke, you just feel free to come home here with Dave or Jilly whenever you like, now won't you?' said Mrs Martin, getting up to make yet another pot of tea.

'Your mother's a nice person, Dave,' began Brooke as Jilly followed her aunt into the kitchen.

Dave came over and sat beside Brooke on the step. 'Brooke, I'm sorry I put you in an embarrassing position before.' He had the grace to look sheepish, even though she could tell he was upset. 'I'm afraid seeing Jacqui here out of the blue kind of threw me and my defence mechanisms took over automatically.' He looked down at his hands. 'You see, Jacqui and I used to be—still are—married.'

'I know. Jilly told me,' Brooke said gently, and then shook her head. 'You know, Dave, Jacqui's to be congratulated. If I'd been in her place I might have brained you and scratched my eyes out.' She tried to add a lighter vein to the conversation.

'She'd have to care one way or another to do that,' said Dave bitterly.

'She wouldn't have called in if she hadn't wanted to see you,' said Brooke.

Dave sighed. 'Maybe. Anyway, I'm sorry I didn't tell you myself that I was married. I don't talk about it much and when a person finds out later I get the feeling they think I've tried to keep it quiet for my own ends. The truth is, it's still an open wound with me.'

'I understand, Dave.' Brooke patted his arm. 'She's a very attractive girl.'

Dave was looking away from her and turned at her words. 'Very,' he said drily, and there was a flash of pain in his dark eyes. 'I know that most of my family and friends lay the blame for our break-up on Jacqui, but I'm afraid it was over fifty per cent my fault. I was one of the best examples of the original male chauvinist pig. I wanted Jacqui at home in an apron, fetching my pipe and slippers, a couple of kids around her feet, always giving me her undivided attention.' He looked self-effacingly at Brooke out of the corner of his eye. 'I suppose you're cringing in your liberated female heart?'

'Not exactly,' she smiled, 'but I can imagine the reactions that statement would create in some circles. For some women that's the rôle in life they need to feel secure, but I can't see your Jacqui being anything other than stifled by it.'

Dave nodded. 'That's what she said at the time, that I was stifling her. We both dug in our heels and didn't talk it over rationally, and the break was inevitable.'

'Do you still feel the same about the apron and the pipe and slippers?'

He laughed softly. 'I guess I've mellowed in my old age.'

'Then why don't you go and tell her so?' suggested Brooke. 'Three years is a long time and old antagonisms can fade.'

'Absence makes the heart grow fonder?' He grinned crookedly. 'I made a bit of a fool of myself tonight, didn't I? But you're right, I should go and see her. I admit that she was the reason I headed home.' He sighed again. 'I don't want to rush it, though. I want us both to be sure this time, no more of the traumas we went through before.'

He leant across and gave Brooke a quick hug. 'Thanks for understanding, Brooke. The trouble is when you've had the real thing you can't settle for anything less.' He laughed selfconsciously. 'Have the bells rung for you yet, Brooke?'

Brooke stiffened beneath his arm, a vivid picture of Kley MacLean springing uninvited into her mind, and her whole expression tensed.

A wave of concern passed over Dave's face. 'Gosh, I'm sorry, Brooke. I'm an unfeeling brute. I was so wrapped up in myself I'd forgotten about. . . . Jilly told me you were once engaged. I hope I haven't upset you. That's the last thing I want to do,' he finished lamely.

Suddenly she was chuckling at his expression. Stephen Marsh seemed, at this moment, decades away. 'No, Dave, it doesn't upset me any more. It's faded into part of the very dim past,' she reassured him. 'And as to the bells ringing—well, I don't think so. Stephen and I drifted into a nice friendly habit that we mistakenly thought was the real thing. Fortunately, the real thing came along for him before we were married. Oh, I was absolutely shattered at the time, I'm not denying that, but now that I can be objective—well, it was all for the best.'

As physically tired as she was after her strenuous and tension-filled day Brooke had considerable trouble getting to sleep that night. Especially since Jilly had received a phone call an hour ago from her parents to say they would be arriving in Townsville the next day on business and wanted her to remain with her aunt for a few extra days. Brooke's stomach had twisted with absolute dread.

They had contacted Kley and now Brooke was travelling to Charters Towers alone. Alone with Kley MacLean, that was. The thought of a morning confined in a small car with Mr High and Mighty did nothing for the state of her nervous system, nor did it soothe her into peaceful sleep.

Jilly's only statement at Brooke's look of horror had been that she was giving Brooke all the opportunities in the world to win her bet.

CHAPTER FIVE

BROOKE's lipstick slipped from her nerveless fingers and fell with a clatter on to the top of her dressing-table. 'Damn!' she said with feeling as she retrieved it before it could roll on to the floor. She'd been dropping things all morning.

Her suitcases were packed and Dave had carried them downstairs and stowed them in the boot of her car. Now she was applying, or trying to apply, a little make-up before joining the others to await Kley's arrival. She glanced at her wristwatch. He would be here any minute now, and she was quaking with the usual feeling of presentiment and she wished the whole day was well and truly behind her.

Angrily she used a tissue to remove a shaky line of colour from her bottom lip and reapplied the pink gloss, pressing her lips together and looking critically at the results in the mirror.

Her outfit wasn't exactly what she would have normally chosen to wear, but her day in the sun had left her skin red and a trifle sore to touch. As a result, for comfort, she had donned a loose pair of light blue slacks and an equally loose white cheesecloth smock. The blouse was soft and sleeveless and didn't irritate her sunburn, and its fullness allowed the air to circulate and cool her tingling skin.

Gathering the last of her things together, she walked slowly downstairs to where Dave was topping up the radiator of her car with water. Mrs Martin and Jilly stepped hurriedly back as he turned the hose on the windscreen, splashing water about with gay abandon.

Catching sight of Brooke, he lifted his hand in a mock salute. 'Your chariot awaits you, mademoiselle.

Suitcases in the boot, guitar case on the back seat in case you feel the urge to serenade Kley en route, petrol, oil, water, battery okay. Windscreen clear,' he grinned. 'All set to go as soon as Kley arrives.'

'Speak of the devil,' remarked Jilly, as Kley swung the Ford into the driveway, spraying gravel back from the tyres.

'You young people, always in a hurry,' remarked Mrs Martin.

'Dead on nine o'clock,' grinned Dave as Kley walked across to Brooke's car with long-legged strides, wishing them all good morning.

He gave Dave the keys to his hired car and dumped his overnight bag on the floor behind the passenger seat of Brooke's car. He raised his eyebrows at the sight of the guitar case on the seat, but although Brooke waited for some derogatory remark from him he made no comment. 'Well, I suppose we'd better head off,' he looked at Brooke. 'Are you ready to go?' His face was set expressionlessly and he moved as though he was holding himself tensely.

Wearing a pair of faded but clean blue denim jeans that hugged his thighs and flared slightly from the knees and a white T-shirt which moulded his muscular chest and shoulders, he looked every bit as fresh and attractive and compelling as he had yesterday, and Brooke felt her jaw clench resolutely. She had to spend roughly two hours with this forceful man, and the sooner it was over the better.

Goodbyes were made and Dave walked around the front of the car with Brooke.

'I'm going to see Jacqui today, so keep your fingers crossed for me,' he said softly, giving her a hug before he opened the door for her to take her seat.

Slightly flushed, she slid behind the steering wheel, but as Kley was already in the car and fixing his seatbelt in place she had no way of knowing whether or not he had witnessed Dave's embrace. Somehow she couldn't imagine his steely eyes missing anything and she could imagine what he was thinking. She buckled herself in and switched on the ignition, backing the car expertly around Kley's car and out on to the road.

They were soon leaving the city and heading along the Charters Towers Road, Kley guiding her through the suburbs, bypassing some of the inner city Monday morning traffic. Out on the open road she slackened her grip on the steering wheel and allowed her taut muscles to relax, trying valiantly to still the fast beat of her heart in its reaction to the nearness of the man beside her.

'How are your muscles today? A little tight?' he broke the silence.

She darted a sideways glance at him, but his eyes were on the road. 'More than a little,' she told him. 'I could barely move when I woke up this morning, but a couple of trips up and down the stairs soon loosened up my muscles for me. Shows how out of condition I am.'

'Your nose is going to peel, too,' he stated matter-of-factly.

One of her hands went gingerly to her nose. 'Does it look so red?' Trust him to point it out, she thought, as she leaned over and glanced quickly in the rear vision mirror, and sat back just as quickly when she realised she had almost leant on him. 'And I thought I'd covered it up reasonably well with warpaint.'

He smiled faintly. 'It's not so obvious really. Your red arms give you away. Did you put some cream or something on your sunburn?'

'Yes, just before I left. Actually it doesn't feel as bad as it looks. It's only the top of my shoulders and my lower back that smart a bit. I suppose you're used to all this fierce sunshine?'

'Mmmm. It's still easy to overdo it. You'll have to remember to wear a hat every time you go outside.' He fell silent.

Brooke sighed. They still had the best part of ninety

kilometres to go and here the conversation had dried up already. For the life of her she couldn't think of anything to say to break the uneasy silence. Maybe if she asked about Terebori Downs?

'So you'll be teaching at the High School along with Dave?' he asked just then, breaking into her thoughts.

'With Jilly and Dave, yes,' she replied quickly.

'That's the school Drew goes to at the moment,' he said thoughtfully.

'Does he? That's great,' she smiled. 'At least I'll have a familiar face among the students to take the edge off the first day, although I may not have him in any of my classes. I won't see very much of Dave as he's in the manual training section and he tells me that's in another building a block or so from the main school, and Jilly's always out on the playing fields.'

His face was still thoughtful and she continued in a rush.

'The first day will be a little nerve-racking for me because I've been lucky enough to be positioned at the one school since I left college. However, I'll soon get into the swing of things, no doubt. The first day's always the worst.'

'You're going to have your work cut out for you,' he said.

'I'm confident of coping,' she replied tensely, feeling a spurt of resentment as she caught a look of cynical disbelief on his face as she glanced sideways at him. She took a deep breath, determined to keep the journey free from any skirmishes, major or minor.

Another silence fell. Brooke looked fleetingly about her. The countryside was dry without being barren and the hardy trees seemed to flourish in that dryness.

'I'm really looking forward to living in the Towers,' she said pleasantly. 'From the little I've read about it, the area oozes history.'

'It does that,' they agreed non-committally.

Brooke tried again. 'Dave tells me that your family

had settled in the area years before the gold rushes began.'

'That's right. A dozen or so years before the rushes in the Towers. My great-great-grandparents, James and Jean MacLean, with their young family, arrived from Scotland with a group of immigrants selected by the Reverend Dr Dunmore Lang, who was an advocate of the free settlers. The family settled firstly in Moreton Bay, but old James wasn't happy there and, around 1860, they left by schooner for Rockhampton.

'This was about the time that exploration of the Burdekin area was being carried out, and when he heard the favourable reports James decided to venture further north. The family then trekked northwards and inland by wagon, driving their small herd of cattle along with them.'

'You can't help but admire them, can you?' she remarked. 'Imagine forging a path through the virgin bush, not knowing what to expect over the next rise or what danger might beset you. It must have been a slow and tedious journey.'

'That's for sure.' He moved slightly to ease his long legs in the confines of the small car. 'Old James decided to put down roots at Terebori Downs because of the spring-fed creek nearby. Water was, and is, always a major factor out here. And, of course, the rainbow,' he pulled a face.

'The rainbow?' she queried.

He laughed softly. 'The story goes, and it's been handed down through the generations, that old James MacLean and his family had been hit by a ferocious thunderstorm as they journeyed north. The rain drenched them in a matter of seconds, and, as they topped a small rise, the sun broke through and they saw a rainbow ending on a hill near a clear-running stream. They decided the rainbow was an omen, and it was on that spot that they built a crude shack and, later, the homestead.'

'I think it's a charming story. You must be proud to be part of it. Why did they call it Terebori Downs?' she asked.

'Terebori in the local aboriginal dialect means rainbow. A very romantic story, isn't it?'

'I think so. I can understand their feelings, coming upon the rainbow after such a long, arduous journey, with the countryside all fresh and clean from the rain,' Brooke sighed. 'Obviously they chose the right place to settle.'

'I guess so, although sometimes it's debatable. Part of the old homestead, incidentally, is still standing and is incorporated in our present house,' he said.

'Did the gold rushes make any difference to those early MacLeans?' Brooke asked him. 'I mean, did they go prospecting, too?'

'By then everything was going along nicely for old James. The homestead was built and the herd had been enlarged,' he continued, 'but when news filtered through to the Downs that two stockmen had discovered gold near Ravenswood station in 1868, James's son, also James, caught the gold fever and, much against his father's wishes, he left the property and set off to make his fortune.'

'And did he find it?'

'Yes, he found it. Twice. And lost it twice. He worked just about every goldfield in the north and was eventually killed in a brawl, of dubious origin, somewhere up near the Palmer River goldfields. He was a bit of a rebel, I'm afraid, but very colourful,' he laughed. 'The youngest son, Andrew, then inherited the Downs, after his mother and the second son died in the typhoid epidemic in the early 1880s. Andrew's son was my grandfather.'

'I don't suppose any gold was ever discovered on the station itself?' Brooke asked.

'Not really. Although my grandfather did do a bit of prospecting on the property, merely as a hobby. The old mine shaft is still intact, but he didn't extract very much gold from the mine.'

By this time they were bypassing the little railway settlement of Mingela and Kley pointed out the road turning off to Ravenswood through what was still dry station country.

'Ravenswood's considered a ghost town now, isn't it?' she asked.

'Just about. A ghost of its former self, anyway. There are about a hundred and thirty people still there. In 1871 there were over forty hotels and licensed shanties in the town. Now there are only two hotels left standing and that's about all. The main street has been taken over by rubber vines and china apple trees.'

'Gold production in that area dropped off before the discoveries were made in the Towers, didn't it?'

'Yes. The reef miners struck trouble with what they called mundic stone—that is, the gold was combined in the ore with copper and zinc, making it very difficult to extract. Later they overcame this with the Scottish cyanide process and the old rubble or mullock heaps were reprocessed very successfully.'

'But Charters Towers saved the day,' remarked Brooke.

'An eleven-year-old aboriginal boy called Jupiter actually discovered the gold while he was searching for runaway horses belonging to three prospectors, Mossman, Clark and Fraser. The find was reported and the rush was immediate, especially as the area was relatively open and pleasant and the gold-bearing quartz was close to the surface. By the end of 1872 there were over three thousand miners working the reefs and while other goldfields came and went the Towers never faltered in its production. By the turn of the century the Towers was really jumping. There were ninety hotels and a population of thirty thousand, and it was known as "The World".'

'I'll bet there are some stories to be told of that era,' said Brooke.

'Very fascinating ones at that,' he replied. 'One story goes that the main street, then Mossman Street, on a Saturday night was reputed to be packed with thousands of people, the successful miners lighting their cigars with ten-pound notes.'

'Ten-pound notes? That would have been a fortune in itself in those days,' she exclaimed.

Kley nodded. 'A brass band would have been playing at each end of the street, each trying to drown out the other, and both vying for dominance over the batteries. And the miners would have been decked out in their best flannel shirts and moleskin trousers, escorting women gaily arrayed with plumes and sporting bustles.'

'And what about the MacLeans out at Terebori Downs?'

'They did very well supplying meat to the town, so I don't think they felt the necessity to dig for gold. Queensland boasted half of the total cattle population in Australia, so times were good on Terebori Downs. The only setback they seemed to have had was the disastrous drought in 1902, but they picked up and kept going.'

'The gold production may be a thing of the past, but I suppose you could say the cattle have gone on for ever,' she smiled. 'It's still the main industry of the area, I believe.'

'For which I'm most thankful,' he half smiled.

By this time the dry, gently undulating country was becoming a little more hilly and Brooke could feel the little car climbing.

'If you slow down now,' Kley said after a short silence, 'you'll see our section of the Burdekin River over the next rise. There's a layby on the hill before the signpost if you'd care to stop for a better look at the view.'

Brooke decelerated and as the little car breasted the rise the panorama of the mighty river lay below them. Flicking on her indicator switch, Brooke veered left into the layby and switched off the engine.

They climbed stiffly from the car, stretching their legs, and from their position on the hilltop the riverbed, at first glance, seemed bone dry, just rocks of various sizes, stunted trees and mile upon mile of reddish cream sand. However, between the gnarled branches of the river gums lining the bank nearest them Brooke could see relatively clear running water. To the left the river was spanned by the huge rail bridge which, Kley informed her, doubled as a road bridge in time of flooding.

The reflected glare of the sun on sand made Brooke wish she hadn't left her sunglasses in the car. 'I guess this is a sight to see when it runs a banker,' she remarked, shielding her eyes with her hand.

Kley nodded and laughed. 'Most of the townsfolk come down for a look-see when it does. There's a real traffic jam on the other side. It's kind of a social event, you might say. Flooding usually occurs in the early months of the year.'

'At the moment it doesn't look like the major coastal river system in the state,' she remarked.

'You'll change your mind if you're still here early next year.'

Somehow the tone he used suggested she wouldn't be, and in a moment of pique she smiled sweetly at him, not looking into his eyes. 'Oh, I'll be here. You just wouldn't believe my staying power!'

'We'll see.' Kley's white teeth flashed as he smiled in the direction of the river, the creases in his tanned cheeks, too masculine to be dimples, deepening with that smile and his eyes crinkling up against the glare.

He really had everything going for him as far as looks were concerned, thought Brooke. Although his features were just that little bit too irregular to be considered handsome in the accepted sense of the word, the ruggedness, combined with the inner strength reflected in his eyes, in the way he held himself, was probably the reason why women stopped to take a second glance. Or even a third, she added to herself, grimacing.

Suddenly she realised her gaze remained on his face, gently mapping out each feature, savouring his attractiveness. Her smile slowly faded as the force of his magnetism flowed through her entire body sparking a flame of awareness, completely overwhelming her.

By sheer willpower alone she forced her gaze back to the river, blind to the scene below her. He was standing so close to her that had she lifted her hand she could touch him, reach out and touch his brown arm, muscularly firm and covered in soft curling brown hair. How would he react if she gave in to the impulse . . .? Good grief, what was the matter with her? She couldn't remember ever so much as contemplating making advances to a man before, let alone this particular man, with his steady stream of conquests. What was she thinking of? She wasn't an inexperienced adolescent.

How could she have even considered making that bet with Jilly? In the light of day, her little essay in revenge seemed futile and trivial. What had Kley MacLean done to her anyway except ruffle her independent feathers? So women fell at his feet, she had just had it made clear to her how easy it would be to follow suit. She would just have to make sure she didn't fall into the same trap.

But still her heart fluttered. She gave herself a mental shake. She wasn't behaving like the Brooke Drynan she knew, was confident of, liked to think was level-headed and in total command of herself. Of course she was level-headed and in command of herself.

Rubbish! snapped an inner voice. You're acting like an infatuated teenager, gazing at the man with adoring eyes. Adoring eyes? Oh, no! Surely she hadn't been doing that! She felt a blush creep up her throat and over her cheeks, making her feel even more wretched.

She let her eyes slide back to the man beside her, expecting his gaze to be on the scene to which she had supposedly been giving her undivided attention. He was looking straight at her and to her embarrassment Brooke felt her blush deepen. Her thoughts skittered about her mind in almost excited confusion as she sensed the air between them crackle with tension.

His thoughts were an enigma to her, the expression in the deep blue depths of his eyes veiled by his long sooty eyelashes. Panic rose within her and she made a move to step backwards, putting a safe distance between them. She was unable to tear her eyes from his face, and as her shoe encountered a patch of uneven ground she stumbled, almost overbalancing.

Kley's strong hands reached out instinctively, clasping her arms. If she thought his nearness before had caused her to tingle with her awareness of him then the extent of her body's reaction to his physical touch shocked her to the very core of her being. She felt dazed, her lips parting as she became slightly breathless.

His fingers moved to her elbows, lingered there, his thumbs gently rubbing her skin, feeling its smoothness, then slid up to her shoulders, drawing her slowly towards him. How many minutes or seconds passed Brooke couldn't have told. Her skin where his fingers had touched seemed to burn as though they had left an indelible path that would remain for ever.

She was totally incapable of tearing her eyes from his, as though, like Narcissus, she was infatuated by her own reflection captured in their blue depths. She knew she should appear outraged, make some effort to push him away before it was too late, before the moment when there would be no going back. In fact, she was absolutely certain that if she did make the slightest move to pull away he would release her immediately and they would go on as though this moment had never happened. Her conscious mind told her this while her physical body showed not the slightest desire to carry out the impulse. No, her traitorous body wanted, yearned, to feel the hard muscular length of his against its own.

His gaze moved down to her lips, taking in their nervous tremble of anticipation, and, with a soft groan of

4 BOOKS AND A SURPRISE GIFT

Here's a sweetheart of an offer that will put a smile on your lips...and 4 free Harlequin romances in your hands. Plus you'll get a secret gift, as well.

As a subscriber, you'll receive 6 new books to preview every month. Always before they're available in stores. Always for less than the retail price. Always with the right to return the shipment and owe nothing.

Please send me 4 **free** Harlequin Romance novels and my **free** surprise gift. Then send me 6 new Harlequin Romances each month. Bill me for only $1.65 each (for a total of $9.95 per shipment — a savings of $1.74 off the retail price) with no extra charges for shipping and handling. I can return a shipment and cancel anytime. The 4 free books and surprise gift are mine to keep!

116 ClR EAXJ

NAME_____

ADDRESS_____APT._____

CITY_____

STATE_____ZIP CODE_____

AS A HARLEQUIN SUBSCRIBER, YOU'LL RECEIVE FREE...

- our monthly newsletter **Heart To Heart**
- our magazine **Romance Digest**
- special-edition **Harlequin Bestsellers** to preview for ten days without obligation

So kiss and tell us you'll give your heart to Harlequin.

protest which seemed to be caught deep in his chest, he pulled her against him and his lips touched hers.

Softly. Feather-soft. Gently. Touching once, twice, until she found herself responding, in spite of herself, to the unexpected gentleness. His arms were around her, tightening, and she was crushed against him, the firmness of his chest against her breasts, the metallic hardness of his belt buckle through the thin cheesecloth of her blouse, the tension in his thighs straining against her own. And as his kisses hardened her lips parted at his practised mastery.

Time stood still for Brooke. No blade of grass waved in the warm breeze, nor leaf fluttered to ground. Her only awareness was this tall, almost stranger. Awareness of his hands as they slid sensually over her back, each movement firing her nerve ends with delightful new sensations, to reach her hips, bringing her impossibly closer into the contours of his body. Awareness of his lips, teasing, probing, seeking a depth and spontaneity of response she never suspected she was capable of, until she thought she would faint with the intensity of it all.

Neither Kley nor Brooke was aware of the rumbling approach of a road train, on its way west, its engine growling with the deep-throated promise of the power needed to haul heavy loads great distances at constant speed. The huge machine drew nearer and eventually attacked the hill, slowing slightly as it climbed the grade. As it topped the rise and started downhill the driver noticed the man and woman locked together and a broad grin split the weatherbeaten face. He gave his loud horn a number of sharp blasts to show his appreciation before he sped down to cross the river, heading homewards.

The blast of the horn vibrated itself into Brooke's consciousness, bringing her back to earth with painful slowness. Her arms had somehow wound themselves about Kley's neck, her fingers twined in his hair. She

dropped her hands to his chest to push herself away
from him, but Kley's arms remained locked around her,
his lips moving down to the hollow of her throat,
almost causing her to drown again in the sensuous feelings he aroused within her. But she firmly continued to
push away until his arms slid reluctantly from her body
and they stood miraculously apart, separate beings
again.

CHAPTER SIX

BROOKE'S entire body seemed not to belong to her and her mind reeled after the emotion-charged moments she had spent in Kley's arms. It must have been a dream, a flight of fancy. But no, the harsh sun was burning on the back of her head and an insect buzzed nearby.

How could she have let herself down like that? So much for her plans to bring him to heel and walk away laughing! Perhaps the point had been proved. She had a terrible suspicion that he had turned the tables on her and that she was about to join the long line of worshippers at his shrine.

What must he be thinking at this moment? That her response to his caresses in such an unrestrained manner gave him carte blanche? That she was fast, one of the frivolous liberated city females who flitted through life without giving moral obligations a second's thought? She was beginning to have grave doubts herself, if it came to that. Or maybe he just accepted her submission as his right?

If he was horrified at her abandoned behaviour, then she was doubly horrified. Never in her wildest dreams had she imagined she would respond to a man's touch the way she had responded to Kley's. And why did it have to be this man, towards whom she had felt so antagonistic? Panic welled up inside her and she had that same urge to escape, to put as much distance as possible between herself and this tall unknown man. But she remained exactly where she was, not able to move.

From behind her lashes she stole a quick glance at him. He was in the act of lighting up a cigarette, the first she had seen him smoke, and almost clinically she noted that his hands cupping the flare of the match were not as steady as she would have expected them to be. A pulse beat in his tightened jaw. Drawing deeply on his cigarette, he exhaled a smoky haze, disguising the expression in his eyes, eyes that she could feel were nevertheless resting upon her, giving not a clue to his reactions.

Brooke blushed anew and the corners of his mouth moved upwards as he grinned ruefully.

'Fate throws a spanner in the works, in the form of a long-distance road train. I guess we'd better get back on the road.' He walked over and opened the driver's side door, holding it open for her to climb back inside.

She watched him walk around the front of the car trying unsuccessfully to gauge his thoughts from the expression on his face. He folded himself into the passenger seat after carefully stubbing out his cigarette on the stony ground. Sighing, she reached out to switch on the ignition as his hand moved out to touch her arm. She gave a start, more from instantaneous response to the feel of his fingers than anything else, her eyes darting back to his face. When his jaw tightened she realised he must have jumped to the wrong conclusions.

'Brooke, I'm not about to attack you, nor am I going to apologise for a kiss.' His voice sounded harsh and louder in the confines of the car.

'I . . . I wasn't going to ask for an apology,' she began haltingly, torturing herself with the realisation that he could describe what had happened between them as 'a kiss'. Perhaps for him it had been only that, a physical thing, to be enjoyed for the moment. Obviously she was making more of it than he was. Perhaps. . . .

'All right,' he said, 'maybe I came on a little strongly, but I get—I got the impression that you enjoyed it as much as I did. God. knows, I've wanted to kiss you since I met you on Saturday night.' He ran his fingers through his hair in exasperation. 'I don't know how I kept my hands off you on the island yesterday. But you knew that, didn't you?' His grimace was all self-mockery. 'That's why you kept your distance.' His eyes travelled down over her body, lingering on the agitated rise and fall of her breast, then moved back to her face.

His eyes had changed colour again, to almost blueblack, and his face held that burningly intense expression which caused Brooke's heart to start fluttering, her breathing to become irregular. Sliding his arm along the back of the seat, his hand on the back of her head, Kley drew her across until his lips touched hers again, pleasingly demanding.

She had no defence against him as a trembling sensation of pure joy rose within her to tingle gloriously throughout her entire body. Only when his lips released hers did her mind reassert itself. The same feeling of panic, as though she were drowning, returned, and he must surely have read the alarm in her eyes.

His own dark eyes seemed to reach down into her very soul; she was losing herself in their depths; and then his gaze broke away and he turned from her.

'I think that proves my point,' he said.

'Proves your point?' she breathed, her heart leaping into her mouth. 'What point?'

'That you weren't averse to my kisses, no matter how much you protest,' he replied arrogantly. 'Which brings me to my second point,' he turned to face her. 'As you seem to need these——' he paused, 'diversions,' I'd like to offer myself as a substitute, a fill-in if you like.'

'A fill-in?' she repeated blankly.

'I'll put it plainly, Brooke. Dave's a good friend of mine and so is his wife, Jacqui. With a little bit of luck, and no distractions,' he looked at her pointedly, 'they may be able to salvage what began as a good marriage. If you need amorous entertainment—well, I've no commitments to anyone, so perhaps I could persuade you to leave Dave and Jacqui to sort themselves out, and I'm sure you and I could have some—er—interesting times.' He smiled confidently.

It was the smile that brought Brooke's rising anger to boiling point, and her hand swung in an arc towards his face. The confines of the car took much of the power from her swing, but still the sound of her hand coming into contact with his cheek echoed around them.

His jaw set and his eyes narrowed with anger as a dull flush suffused his cheek where she had hit him. For a split second she thought he was going to hit her back, but his clenched hand fell back on to his lap.

Brooke recoiled in disbelieving horror at her actions. She had never raised a hand to anyone, not even her most troublesome students had caused her to lose her temper so violently. What was happening to her? She took a deep breath.

'I'm sorry, I shouldn't have done that,' she said softly, 'but you must admit I was provoked.'

'At least we know where we stand,' Kley said at last. 'But my warning regarding Dave still goes. Keep away from him, Brooke, and let them work out their problems alone.'

'I'm not. . . .' Brooke gave in. 'Oh, what's the use!'

'My sentiments exactly. I think it would be as well if we pushed on,' he added firmly.

In a daze of still burning anger and resentment Brooke pulled back on to the highway, down the incline and across the long, low Macrossan Road Bridge over the Burdekin River, up the rise on the other bank and back through the seemingly never-ending dried grass, thin native bushes and china apple trees. The sooner they arrived in the Towers the better she would like it.

They travelled in that same strained silence until a few far from new houses came into sight on not very prosperous-looking properties, fenced by stranded barbed wire. The buildings themselves had in common their high-pitched corrugated iron roofs, latticed verandahs, peeling paintwork and leaning outhouses.

However, by the time a signpost proclaimed that they had entered Charters Towers proper, the houses were tidier, the gardens trimmed, although the grass didn't appear to be that much greener than it had been along the roadside.

Putting the man beside her from her mind, Brooke drove slowly, taking the opportunity to glance quickly about her with interest, forming her first impressions of the city. Somehow she had expected a flat, dry, dusty township, but this was far from the case. She was surprised at the abundance of trees. They grew everywhere, tall gums, cultivated bushes alongside natives, poincianas and shady spreading tamarinds.

'Take the next turn left, by the motel,' Kley spoke for the first time. 'Behind the trees on your left is Lissner Park.'

The park was to Brooke an oasis in the desert. The carpet-like grass was almost green, greener than any she had seen since Townsville. Twirling sprays of irrigating water threw rainbows in the sunlight. The same huge tamarind trees stood alongside ancient gums and a small bandstand, its shining red roof and white lace-patterned wrought ironwork, added a splash of colour to the muted greens.

Kley guided her to the right where the street forked at an old two-storied hotel-like building which he told her used to be just that. The Park Hotel was a fine example of tropical architecture. It was surrounded by copious verandahs with shutters and adjustable louvres to regulate the breeze and keep out the burning sunlight. On the roof galvanised ventilators whirled in the breeze.

'Oh, Mossman Street.' Brooke read the sign. 'This is where the miners used to light their cigars with ten-pound notes,' she exclaimed, forgetting her earlier coolness in her excitement.

'Among other things. If you pull over here you can take your time looking over the street,' Kley said evenly.

Yes, if one used just a smidgen of imagination the

whole street came alive to the revelry of the miners. They would have been hard workers and equally hard players. Brooke could almost hear the bands, the laughter, the clank of the batteries.

'The large charcoal grey building with the white trim is the Australian Bank of Commerce,' Kley's voice brought her back to the twentieth century, 'which is basically Renaissance style with the usual adaption for the tropics, especially in the use of open colonnades.

'Just behind that and further along, the rather strikingly coloured pale blue and white building is the City Hall, also Renaissance. In fact, it was originally built as a bank. Most bank buildings at that time had leanings towards the Renaissance, but a more three-dimensional effect has been created by the deep patios and verandahs.'

'What's the cream-coloured building with the small semi-circular roof over the entrance? The one up the end on the same side of the street?' she asked.

'That's the old Stock Exchange. It's been restored and houses a museum and is well worth a visit.'

The entire street was a fascination, thought Brooke, a slice out of the past. Two-storied concrete buildings rubbed shoulders with single storied ornate businesses, their roofs continuing over the footpath, some well kept, others decaying and rundown. She was so enchanted her earlier anger had been pushed to the back of her mind.

'What a fantastic place! I didn't imagine anything so . . . so steeped in history.'

Kley looked over the street with the acceptance of a native and shrugged his shoulders. 'There are a few places that are only fit to be condemned, but I guess we wouldn't change the old place.'

He glanced at his wristwatch. 'As it's about lunch time, would you care to join me for a counter lunch before you begin moving into your flat?'

She looked at him in surprise.

'Look, Brooke, I think we should try to put our—

er—differences behind us. This is an isolated town and we'll be running into each other consistently, so I suggest we're civil to each other at least.' He looked straight at her. 'Besides, I would like to show my appreciation for the lift.'

'Didn't you say you wanted to be back at the station by lunch time?' she asked, playing for time.

He shrugged his shoulders again. 'The station's managed without me for nearly a week, so an extra hour or two won't upset the applecart.' When she still hesitated he said a little shortly, 'Yes or no, Brooke. No strings attached.'

'All right. Thank you very much. Which way do we go?' A small voice demanded why she hadn't refused his offer out of hand, but she ignored it, pulling the car back on to the road again.

'Left into Gill Street,' he said. 'This is now the main street. The large building with the clock tower is the Post Office, which is fairly typical of the post offices built at that time.'

Brooke slowed down. 'What's that unusual building opposite?'

'The Stan Pollard and Company Store. I guess you'd call it Art Nouveau. You either love it or hate it.'

The building itself was very symmetrical, with two octagonal towers supporting a huge arch. The boarding to the street in its own zigzag pattern boldly told the contents of the store, from hosiery to millinery, men's wear to crockery.

'This particular section of the street was used in the making of the film *The Irishman*. The townsfolk still talk about it and probably will for decades to come. Some of them even played the thousand screaming extras,' he laughed. 'The street was covered with gravel from gutter to gutter, the cast appeared in period costume and you would have sworn you'd tumbled down a time tunnel and the years had slipped away.'

'Did you have a part in the film?' Brooke asked,

tongue in cheek, as they continued down through the shopping area, past chemists, newsagents, cafés, large and small stores, all painted with the brush of bygone days. The only jarring note was the modern tavern at the bottom of the main street.

'No, not me,' Kley smiled as they drove slowly up the other rise, not taking her bait. 'There's a parking space up ahead.'

Brooke pulled into the high curb.

'I thought we'd have lunch across the road in the Excelsior Hotel, if you have no objections. I'm afraid we don't boast a restaurant, only two or three cafés, and I always feel the food is better here. The pub has survived its century and it's one of the diminishing number of hotels still in existence from the gold rush days.'

They crossed the street to the imposing hotel. The two-storied building seemed to glitter, its deep upstairs verandahs featuring a simple crisscross balcony rail detail. The broad footpaths along the street were covered by the overhanging verandahs, supported on delicate cast-iron columns with some patterned iron lace hanging like half curtains to the street.

Kley held open the mirrored swinging door into the lounge and as they entered the cool dining room, Brooke felt she was stepping back decades. She had barely taken stock of her surroundings, the dark polished floor, the varnished wooden walls, when she became aware that they were the object of all eyes. Not that the gazes turned on her were in any way offensive, in fact, quite the reverse, and she felt herself flush. It seemed that a new face was something of a novelty.

The sight of Kley MacLean escorting an unknown young woman was just as much of a novelty to the locals as Brooke's new face, but that was a thought which didn't even cross her mind. A few hands were raised in friendly recognition of the man at her side and one or two of the men called greetings, all of which

Kley acknowledged without seeking any further conversation. He held out a chair for her at a table by the window and her flushed face welcomed the cooling breeze encouraged through the open window by a spinning overhead fan.

'What would you like to drink?' he asked, standing by the table, looking down at her.

'Perhaps a light shandy,' she replied quickly.

He nodded his head and she watched his broad back as he walked to the bar opening between the lounge and the public bar.

She took a hurried glance once again at their audience only to find the men's attention had returned to the game of football being shown on the colour TV set over the bar. Even Kley watched the play as he waited for their drinks.

All the occupants of the lounge shared one common denominator. To a man they wore sturdy faded jeans or khaki drill trousers which fitted close to their ankles, some tucked tidily into the tops of high-heeled riding boots, others left to wrinkle over the tooled leather boots.

And they all possessed large-brimmed hats, resting on bended knees, on the bar top, tucked under arms, all well worn and fingered, brim angles reflecting their owners' personal preferences. Shirts of various colours were rolled up over muscular brown forearms.

Kley returned with two frosted glasses and sat down in the chair beside Brooke, his back to the room. She took a welcome sip of the cold pale amber liquid and hurriedly set her glass down as he passed her the luncheon menu. Suddenly her appetite deserted her. Here she was, sitting in a strange hotel with a man who had less than an hour ago stirred her senses more than any man had ever done, who had insulted her in a way no man had ever done, and yet who now seemed determined to make a pretence at civilised conversation as though none of it had happened.

'A new face is always of interest here,' he said softly at last. 'But you won't find anyone rude enough to continue staring just for the sake of it. These boys are on their lunch break from the cattle yards. Now, how about the chicken salad? Or would you prefer something hot?'

Brooke relaxed and shook her head. 'No, the salad will be fine, thank you.'

He went to the counter to order their lunch and a short time later a very young waitress brought their meal over to them, turning a beaming face on Kley.

'Hello, Kley.' She cast a curious glance at Brooke. 'We don't often see you here in the middle of the day.'

Kley rewarded her with his best smile. And the girl was not unmoved by it, thought Brooke disgustedly.

'How are things, Jody?' he asked.

'Fine,' the girl beamed, and looked at Brooke again so that Kley was forced to introduce them.

'Brooke will be teaching up at the High School next term,' he told the other girl.

'Another teacher, hey? I wonder how long she'll last?' laughed Jody, turning back to Kley. 'I really don't know how anyone can bear being cooped up with thirty or forty little hooligans.'

Brooke smiled sweetly, refusing to look at Kley. 'It has its moments,' she said, thinking wryly that this girl wasn't long past the hooligan stage herself.

'Yes, well, I must get back to work. Good to see you again, Kley,' and with a half smile in Brooke's direction she left them to their lunch.

'Jody's brother works on the Downs. She's a nice kid,' remarked Kley.

'I'm sure she is,' said Brooke evenly.

They chatted lightly throughout the meal, keeping to neutral subjects, although they were neither of them unaware of the currents that still flowed beneath the surface.

'What made you want to come up north to teach?'

Kley asked, lighting a cigarette, his eyes narrowed against the curl of smoke.

'I just wanted a change of scene,' she replied, 'and from what I've seen it looks like I'm going to get it.'

He drew on his cigarette. 'No broken hearts left behind in the Big Smoke?'

She hesitated a little before shaking her head, and although he made no comment she knew he had noticed her slight pause before she answered.

'Hardly. I'm afraid it was nothing more exciting than the urge to climb out of my rut.'

He regarded her with amused scepticism, which rubbed her the wrong way. 'I find it hard to believe that someone as attractive as you are could have been left alone in a rut.'

Brooke felt her teeth clench, all her previous antagonisms associated with this man rising up to flash in her eyes. Forcing herself to remain calm, she looked him unflinchingly in the eyes and smiled again. 'Thank you for the compliment,' she said, tongue in cheek. We both know you weren't being complimentary, Mr High and Mighty, she thought. 'I guess I mustn't have appealed to the southern men. Perhaps it's a case of one man's meat being another man's poison, so maybe I'll have more luck up here in the north.' She raised her eyebrows enquiringly.

His eyes moved from her face, slowly down her smooth column of throat which his lips had caressed so convincingly not long before. 'You might, at that,' he said enigmatically.

They walked out of the hotel almost into the arms of a short, fair-haired woman, a bag of groceries tucked under each arm, hurrying purposefully along the street. Kley rescued the large bag before it was dropped to the pavement.

'Oh, Kley, I am sorry! I was so intent on racing home that I didn't see you there.' The woman smiled apologetically, her bright eyes glancing at Brooke with interest.

'You should have had these groceries delivered for you, Ann, instead of carting them around in this heat.' Kley relieved her of the other bag.

'I was in such a hurry to get back and I just had to have these few things. I'm expecting my new tenants today and I've been hoping against hope that they won't arrive before I get home. I do want to be there to welcome them properly. They're two young teachers from Brisbane.'

'All your problems are solved, Ann,' Kley smiled. 'Allow me to introduce one of your new tenants. Brooke Drynan, meet Ann Mason.'

Ann Mason smiled and held out her hand in surprise. 'My dear, how do you do? Welcome to the Towers. I'm so glad you arrived safely. Do excuse my ravings, but I'm such a ditherer when I'm rushing about. My husband always tells me to put out my hand to make sure where I am. Didn't your friend arrive with you?'

'No. Jilly stayed on in Townsville to see her parents. She won't be here for a few days,' Brooke told her. 'At least you won't have to walk home, Mrs Mason, we can kill two birds with the one stone.' She smiled as Kley led them across to where her car was parked. 'I can give you a lift home and you can give me directions to my flat.'

Stowing the groceries behind the back seat, Kley lifted out his bag. 'Well, ladies, I'll leave you to it. Thanks for the lift, Brooke. I certainly appreciated it.'

'We can drop you off on our way, can't we?' asked Brooke, perversely not wanting to see him go.

'She'll be right,' he assured her. 'You go a block that way,' he pointed up the side street, 'and I go a couple of blocks in the opposite direction. It won't take me long to walk down to Aunt Peg's and collect my utility. I'll be out to the Downs in no time.'

Brooke's heart sank inexplicably. 'Thank you for the lunch. It was most enjoyable. Oh, and thanks for showing me around the township.'

'No worries.' He touched the brim of his hat, which he had taken from the back of the car, with one finger and paused before he added, 'I'll see you both around.' And he walked off down the hill with long purposeful strides.

'Well, I guess we can be off.' Brooke dragged her eyes from Kley's retreating figure and forced a bright note into her voice. They climbed into the car for the last leg of Brooke's sixteen-hundred-kilometre journey.

'Fancy you knowing Kley MacLean,' remarked Ann Mason as Brooke pulled away from the curb.

'Well, actually, I don't know him very well at all,' she hoped her voice sounded normal. And I wish I'd never met him, she added to herself. 'I drove up from Brisbane with two of his friends and he needed a lift back to the Towers, so it fitted in very well.'

Ann's curiosity seemed to be satisfied. 'On the corner there, Brooke,' she broke off to point out their destination. 'The garage for your flat is the one with the white door. We're in the highset house next door.'

They delivered the groceries to Ann's house and she collected the flat key.

'I've had the windows open all morning, so it shouldn't be stuffy. There, what do you think?' She stepped back to let Brooke inside.

The door opened from the landing straight into a long rectangular room, a combined living room, dining room and kitchen area. Three gaily coloured floral easy-chairs were arranged around a circular fluffy rug on the polished wood floor. A small table and two chairs, for dining, were pushed to one wall and the living-dining area was divided from the kitchen area by a set of cupboards, the top of which formed a breakfast bar. Underneath stood two lime green stools. The kitchen was neat and compact with the cupboards painted rich cream with bright green formica bench tops. The floor was covered in autumn-toned vinyl.

'It's lovely,' said Brooke sincerely, and Ann's face broke into a smile.

'Come and see the rest,' she trotted across to the door in the opposite wall. 'The bedroom's through here.'

It was a reasonably large room containing two large wardrobes, a dressing-table and twin beds covered with colourful Indian weave spreads. The tiny shower and toilet opened off the bedroom.

'Do you think you'll like it?' asked Ann anxiously.

'I love it already,' Brooke exclaimed. 'And so will Jilly. She'll only be here for a couple of months and then I'll be on my own. As soon as our trunks arrive by rail we'll have the place looking like home in no time.'

'Did you bring very much with you?' asked the other woman.

'No, not much. Only my bookcase and a couple of beanbag chairs. I wasn't sure how much space I'd have, so I thought I'd just bring a few things and my parents could despatch anything else I needed.'

'Very sensible, too,' nodded Ann. 'Well, I'll leave you to it. If you need any help I'll be next door.' She went towards the door. 'Oh, pop over at about three-thirty for an afternoon cuppa.'

She ended up having dinner with the Masons, Ann's husband being the principal of the school where Brooke was to teach. Although they had a very enjoyable evening Brooke was loath to touch on the subject of the difficult students at the high school and John Mason made no mention of it, so Brooke decided it couldn't be as bad as it was reputed to be.

It was well after eleven o'clock by the time she fell into bed and, even though her body was exhausted after her long and tiring day, her mind was over-active. Thoughts and impressions chased about in her head while she yearned for the release of a deep and dreamless sleep.

Persistently it was thoughts of Kley MacLean that rose before her, the vividness of the pictures overshadowing all other impressions. The deep dark blue of his eyes, the breadth of his muscular shoulders and the strength in his arms as they bound her to him, the heady sensation of his body pressed so close to her own. Now, her body burned, as those moments returned so graphically that he was almost real enough to touch.

However, his derogatory words that followed those moments also returned to humiliate her once more and, groaning, she turned restlessly on to her back in the unfamiliar bed. What was she going to do about his erroneous opinion of her? Did she care enough to want to change his impression of her, that was more to the point? The fact that a lot of his misjudgement was of her own making didn't help to settle her chaotic thoughts at all.

She could have sworn the attraction she had felt in his arms had been genuinely reciprocated, but apparently it wasn't, and that kind of physical relationship she could do without at this time.

Determinedly Brooke forced it from her mind and began resolutely to count sheep that turned into cattle and then horsemen, tall, dark horsemen who all looked remarkably familiar.

CHAPTER SEVEN

CROSSING the school ground towards 'B' block and the staffroom she was to share with five of her fellow teachers, including Jilly, Brooke couldn't control the flutter of butterflies in the pit of her tummy. The school secretary had directed her to the upper floor of 'B' block and she was aware of the glances of curiosity on the faces of the milling students as she passed by.

She was a new face, as yet an unknown quantity, although she knew that at least half of the student body would by now be aware of her full christian names and that, given until the close of school that day, they would all know the name of her last school, how long she had been there and most probably her date and place of birth. It was quite amazing how rapidly the word got around.

Smiling to herself, she caught a glimpse of a familiar dark head a few paces in front of her and, lengthening her stride, she reached out and touched Drew on the shoulder. 'Hi, Drew,' she smiled. 'I was hoping I'd catch up with you some time today.'

Drew's mouth had fallen open in amazement, but he quickly recovered himself, glancing sideways at two other boys who had stopped when he did. 'Oh, hi, Brooke. What are you doing here? I didn't expect to see you. . . .' He stopped short, his eyes widening as the truth dawned on him. 'Hey, you're not one of our new . . .? You can't be. . . .'

Brooke laughed at his expression. 'One of the establishment, I have to admit.'

'Gosh, when Dave said you were a teacher I never thought you'd be teaching here.' Drew still looked stunned.

'Aren't you a second-former?' Brooke asked.

Drew nodded.

'Not 2AB, by any chance?'

Drew nodded again.

'Well, I'm your new form teacher,' Brooke informed him.

If it was possible Drew looked even more taken aback. 'You're our new form teacher?' he repeated slowly, a multitude of expressions crossing his face. 'But ... but you can't be! Not you.'

'I'm afraid I am,' she told him. 'What makes you think it's so impossible? I can be a bit of an old dragon when aroused,' she teased him.

'But we've always had ... well, you're a girl,' he finished lamely. 'We've always had a man for our form teacher.'

'Until now you have,' replied Brooke as the bell rang to indicate that it was ten minutes to assembly. 'Well, I won't hold you up. Besides, I must rush my things up to the staffroom. See you later, Drew. Boys.' She smiled at Drew's friends. As she turned to mount the stairs she noticed that Drew was still standing staring after her with a worried frown on his face.

Three of her new colleagues were in the staffroom when Brooke hurried in and they greeted her woefully, decrying the fact that today meant back to the grind. Brooke had already been introduced to them and they showed her which desk she could use.

'I feel a real heel about you being landed with 2AB, Brooke,' said Peter Malpass, a pleasant fair-haired young man whose wife taught domestic science. 'Perhaps it would be as well if I swapped with you and you could take my form, 1A. How about it?'

'No, thanks, Peter. It's okay, honestly. I'm replacing Frank Dennis and 2AB was his form. If we start changing around now the roster is going to go haywire.' Brooke looked at the three faces, all displaying pitying expressions. 'Surely the 2AB's can't be so bad, can they?'

Peter and the other two teachers exchanged knowing looks and spoke in unison. 'They're worse!'

'They are somewhat unmanageable—and that's an understatement. Not that they're all bad,' Peter added. 'As usual you have a ringleader, or in the case of 2AB, you have two ringleaders with a couple of lesser stirrers who incite the rest of the class to riot.'

'Who are these ringleaders I should be wary of?' Brooke asked, feeling a quiver of apprehension.

'One Andrew Bastien, the form captain, and his mate, Joey West. Both intelligent kids, but a trifle misguided,' Peter pulled a face. 'I'm sure I don't know what the Boss is thinking about saddling you with that lot.' Peter shook his head.

The Boss, they explained to Brooke, was the title given to the principal, John Mason, by both teachers and students alike, although no one could quite remember how or why the nickname had been coined.

Peter Malpass levered himself off the desk top on which he had been sitting. 'I'll go along and check 2AB's home room. The little perishers have a habit of booby-trapping the room as a welcome to new teachers.'

'Booby-traps?' Brooke raised her eyebrows. 'What sort of booby-traps? Tacks on chairs? Things like that?' She became even more uneasy, also wondering if John Mason knew what he was about setting her such a troublesome class.

'Among other things,' grimaced Peter. 'Frank Dennis had a balloon of water fall on him when he opened the classroom door. Oh, and incidentally, the door knob had been coated with Vaseline. That was just for starters. Poor bloke was a nervous wreck by the end of the first week. He wasn't a very forceful type of fellow to begin with, so you can imagine what a field day the little horrors had. Anyway,' Peter ambled towards the door, 'I'll go and give the room a quick check over. See you at assembly.'

As the three girls made their way to the school parade ground for the first morning assembly of the new term, Kate and Penny, the Domestic Science teachers, also tried to convince Brooke that she should change her mind about swapping classes with Peter. Some four hundred students scurried about sorting themselves into some kind of order.

A few moments before the final bell rang Peter materialised beside Brooke. All three girls looked at him expectantly and he shrugged his shoulders.

'Clean as a whistle. No water bomb. No tacks on the chair. The door knob's a bit tacky, so I'd say it's been wiped clean. I can't understand it,' he frowned. 'I still don't trust them, so be careful, won't you, Brooke?' he added as the deputy principal called for silence.

At the end of assembly Brooke moved briskly to her home room, knowing she had a few moments' start on her class. They would be an unusual class indeed if they hurried to their room on the first day of the new semester.

The classroom at the end of the second floor of 'B' block was basically the same as all other classrooms in which she had taught. There were rows of desks to seat the thirty boys who comprised 2AB. The class actually consisted of a third A's, those taking a majority of academic subjects, and two thirds B's, those who combined technical subjects with the normal academic subjects.

To one side of the room stood a sturdy locker which housed equipment used specifically by 2AB and out in the front stood what was to be Brooke's own desk. She quickly checked out the drawers of the desk and her chair for any sign of tampering as she listened for the sound of the boys moving along the verandah.

The wall behind her desk was almost all blackboard. There were two boards set on a pulley system whereby one board could be raised and the other was automatically lowered. At the moment one board was behind the other, both resting halfway up the wall.

Sighing, Brooke moved towards the doorway as the first of the boys began lining up outside. She gave the blackboards a final glance and her eye was caught by the edge of the blackboard duster resting precariously across the top of the two blackboards. It was an old trick. When one blackboard was pulled down the oblong duster was dislodged to fall on the unsuspecting person beneath.

She muttered grimly to herself. It was too late to remove it now. She put a smile on her face as she motioned the boys to file into their seats. Drew didn't meet her eye as he went to his desk in the back row, just off to her left. One of the boys who had been with him this morning was sitting beside him.

While the boys settled down, their faces placidly angelic, Brooke opened the daily roll. Her eyes flew down the list of names and she frowned slightly. No MacLean was listed. Of course, she told herself, Drew wasn't a MacLean. He was Kley's sister's child. She hadn't given that a thought. He had seemed all MacLean somehow.

Smiling, she introduced herself to the class and asked each boy to stand as she called his name from the roll so that she could begin to get to know everyone. She was especially interested to make the acquaintance of Andrew Bastien, the troublemaker. There were three names before his, John Allen and Peter and Paul Andrews, who turned out to be identical twins sporting fiery red hair and freckled faces.

'Andrew Bastien.' Brooke looked up quickly and felt her breath catch in her throat as a tall dark-haired boy in the back row stood up. Drew? It couldn't be. She finished the roll call in something of a daze. Drew and Andrew Bastien, the rebel, were one and the same. But Drew had seemed such a pleasant young boy, a trifle precocious but very likeable all the same. How could he be the uncontrollable larrikin he was reputed to be? She did recall being told that Kley had had some trouble with Drew at school, but she hadn't put two and two together. Andrew shortened to Drew. It was quite a shock.

But now she would have to give the class the changes in their daily subject timetable. That meant it was time to use the blackboard, and the duster was going to take a neat piece of precision fielding. Brooke moved over towards the blackboard, turning her back on the class. There was the box of chalk on the ledge at the base of the blackboard frame. As she reached out to select a piece of chalk a movement in the box caught her eye, and it was all she could do to stop herself jumping back a couple of paces.

A bleary eye gazed up at her from the most ugly and grotesque of shapes. A brown cane toad, larger than the ones she had occasionally come across down south but fortunately not as large as the ones she had seen at Dave's place in Townsville. The thought that she had come close to actually touching one made her feel quite faint.

Becoming aware of the whole class waiting expectantly for her reaction, she pulled herself shakily together. This would take all the self-control she could muster. With a hand that shook slightly in spite of itself she picked up the thick yellow cloth duster and, putting it over the toad, she lifted the creature from the box before she had second thoughts and turned back to the class.

The toad, almost as startled as Brooke had been, made one futile clutch at the air with a stubby front leg and then remained immobile, which was rather providential, Brooke thought wryly. Had the toad wriggled convulsively she would have dropped the unfortunate creature and run for her life.

'One volunteer to remove our visitor.' Her best Miss Drynan voice scarcely wavered.

The boys eyed the toad in Brooke's hand, some with surprised admiration. One of the red-haired Andrews twins bounded forward, a grin from ear to ear. 'Yes, miss, where will I put it?'

'How about where it came from?' Brooke deposited the toad thankfully into the boy's outstretched hands, shuddering inwardly.

'Aw, miss, how would I know where it came from? I didn't put it there—honest!' The freckled face was all hurt affront.

'Yes, I know,' Brooke couldn't help smiling at him, 'not one of you would even contemplate putting a toad in the chalk box. Now take it downstairs, and be quick about it.'

She was relieved to see the toad go, deciding she wouldn't be able to look at another chalk box without a shudder of unease. 'Now, let's get down to our weekly syllabus. I'll write the changes down on the blackboard and you can all make a copy. I believe there are a number of changes from last semester.' Brooke dug a piece of chalk from the bottom of the chalk box. Now for the falling duster epic. Timing was most important.

There was a cough and shuffling from the back of the room and, glancing back towards the class, she noticed that Drew was looking decidedly unhappy. He raised his eyes to the duster emphatically, in an effort to warn her, but Brooke steeled herself. If Drew was the instigator of all the trouble it would do him good to suffer a little. She took her time, shuffling her papers into order before walking across and reaching up to take hold of the outside blackboard.

'Miss Drynan, excuse me,' Drew's voice came from the back of the room.

Brooke half turned, her hand still on the board. 'Yes, Drew? What is it?'

'Oh . . . that is . . .' his face was pink, 'I need to sharpen my pencil.' He started along the aisle between the desks to where the sharpener was attached to the wall near where Brooke stood.

'All right, but be sure to sharpen your pencils before class next time.' And Brooke gently pulled the board down with her left hand and with her right hand caught the falling duster neatly.

Drew had reached the sharpener and had the grace to blush and give her an apologetic lopsided grin.

'The fairies again, I suppose?' She faced the class and gave them a friendly but firm lecture concerning the disruption of her lessons.

The next uneventful hour before morning break she spent assessing the progress the class had made in the subjects she was to teach them. She was appalled at the amount of work that remained to be done before the end of the semester. Amid cries of woe and some stony stares she informed them that they would have to put their noses to the grindstone to catch up.

The days flew by and Brooke found herself exhausted by the time she fell into bed each night. Never before had a class proved such a challenge, and not for ages had she felt so vitally alive. Little by little she seemed to be gaining the upper hand with 2AB, although how much of that upper hand was due to her teaching abilities and how much importance was owed to the fact that Drew was on her side she couldn't hazard a guess. But they seemed to be responding.

And their response was a source of complete amazement to the other members of the teaching staff. Peter Malpass suggested that she obviously had them under some form of hypnotic spell, while Kate O'Brien, a dyed-in-the-wool Women's Libber, stated that it could only be another show of the superiority of the female of the species.

About a fortnight after the recommencement of school Brooke had discovered that the class had been banned from participation in all school sporting activities because of their consistently disruptive behaviour. She managed to convince John Mason that the boys deserved a second chance, and surprisingly they hadn't let her down. Now, at least half of the class was involved in school sporting teams. Drew was now in training for the inter-school swimming competitions. This caused even further amazement among her fellow teachers, who grudgingly reported to Brooke that her boys were also vastly improved in the classes not under her jurisdiction. Jilly and Dave Martin said they couldn't understand what all the fuss was about, 2AB were no better or worse than any other class of teenage boys.

Jilly and Brooke were settling in well together in their flat and Dave was a regular visitor during the week. Quite often Jilly was out and he would sit chatting to Brooke for ages, mostly about Jacqui and the improvement in their relationship. He journeyed to Townsville each weekend and they were seeing each other regularly, without rushing blindly into any reconciliations. Although she liked Dave Brooke was beginning to think wryly that he was using her as a sounding board for his troubles.

If Kley MacLean came to know of Dave's innocent visits he would be far from pleased, but she wasn't answerable to him, so why should she worry. And if he chose to think the worst of her then that was his loss. Only occasionally did Dave or Drew mention him, and then only to report that he was very busy on the Downs, either herding, branding or dipping cattle.

In her first few days with her class Brooke had come to realise that the more conventional teaching methods were usually met with resistance and aggression, and she found herself continually pitting her wits against the boys'. However, just when she felt she should throw in the towel they would surprise her by responding to what would be a 'desperation' idea on her part.

After one particularly trying period of history her temper had begun to fray around the edges, and that night she prowled around the flat trying to decide which tack to take with the boys this time. Jilly was visiting an old school friend and wouldn't be home until late. Up till now Brooke had coaxed rather than played the heavy teacher and she wondered if she had been doing the right thing. Had she been too lax with them? The problem tossed about in her mind until she switched on the television set in the hope that she would be able to relax and banish 2AB from her thoughts completely for a few hours.

A racy detective show couldn't hold her attention and eventually she flicked the off switch and stretched out full length on her large beanbag chair, reaching exasperatedly for her transistor radio. It crackled and spluttered as she moved the dial. A soft ballad issued forth, a group singing in harmony backed by mellow guitars.

Brooke sighed appreciatively. The ballad told the tale of a poor soul wrenched from the bosom of his family and transported to the dreaded penal colony of New South Wales. The programme continued with more folk tunes, each telling its own story. Like a page from a history book, mused Brooke, and sat bolt upright, her transistor clutched in her hand.

Like a page from a history book. Of course! She should have thought of it before. It was worth a try—anything was worth a try. Excitedly she found her case of sheet music and reached to the bottom for her old collections of folk songs and began searching through the titles. She hadn't even glanced at them since her college days.

The clock in the next flat, a loudly chiming variety, doggedly announced it was midnight before she became aware that her cramped position on the floor had cut off circulation to her legs. She set aside her guitar with satisfaction and rubbed her protesting muscles. To one side was a discarded stack of manuscripts and she lifted the eight pieces she had chosen depicting life in penal Australia. She would take her guitar along tomorrow and use the songs to illustrate her history lesson on that same subject.

With a smile of anticipation she tidied away her

music and replaced her guitar safely in its case just as Jilly arrived home.

'I hope the little darlings appreciate all your trouble, Brooke,' Jilly said, shaking her head when she heard Brooke's intentions. 'Most teachers would just tell them to shape up or be laid waste.'

Brooke laughed and Jilly looked thoughtfully at her. 'Perhaps the powers that be did know what they were doing for once when they gave you that particular class to tame.'

'They're all basically great kids, Jilly, and I enjoy working with them. It was a stroke of luck that I got to know Drew on the island because it gave me a head start with the class. Drew's a born leader and the others follow his directions. But they're all willing to learn especially if I use a different approach,' she smiled. 'Hence the guitar.'

'And maybe they needed someone who genuinely cared about them,' said Jilly and Brooke laughed again.

'Oh, by the way, before I forget,' remarked Jilly. 'I meant to tell you Kley rang up earlier while you were over at Ann's.' She casually watched for Brooke's reactions through her lashes.

Outwardly the other girl's expression barely altered, although her fingers moved a little agitatedly, smoothing the light material of her printed cotton brunch coat.

'Oh. What did he want?' Brooke managed to say evenly, while her heart seemed to leap in her breast. She had thought these few weeks without seeing Kley would have been long enough to moderate her response to him, but it seemed in this she was wrong.

'He was looking for Dave,' Jilly was saying. 'I wonder why he thought Dave would be here?' she grinned impishly.

Brooke's mouth tightened. Oh, she knew very well why he would try here first.

'If your look could kill!' Jilly's grin widened and she

chuckled. 'What exactly did happen between you two on the trip to the Towers? You never did say much about it.'

'There wasn't much to tell,' replied Brooke, her colour rising despite her offhand tone.

'Then why are you blushing?'

'Jilly Martin, you missed your calling. You should have been a detective,' Brooke half laughed.

'Well, are you going to keep me in suspense, with my imagination running riot?' appealed Jilly. 'I'd say it had something to do with Dave somewhere along the line. Dave with respect to you, that is.'

Brooke sighed. 'Sherlock Holmes, eat your heart out! You're persistent, if nothing else, Jilly.' Her eyes returned to her hands. 'He warned me to keep away from Dave in the most insulting, rude. . . . As if I'd be interested in Dave. I mean, he's nice, Jilly, but. . . .'

'Mmmm. It's as plain as the nose on your face that Dave's still barmy over Jacqui—although why I don't know—so why would Kley think that you and Dave could possibly be romantically involved?'

Brooke could almost see Jilly's agile mind turning over.

'That's it!' she exclaimed at last. 'He's jealous. That's the only reason he could have for warning you off Dave. He fancies you and doesn't want any other guys on the scene. I told you so, didn't I? At the party?'

'Pure fantasy, Jilly,' Brooke shook her head. 'If what you say is true,' a tiny tingling teased the lower regions of her stomach, 'then why has he been conspicuous by his absence? Your theory won't hold water, I'm afraid.'

'That's as well may be, but you mark my words,' Jilly shook one finger at her friend, 'the great man is jealous.' She smiled knowingly and then looked ruefully at Brooke. 'What am I so happy about? Not only do I dip out on the dishiest catch in the country but it looks like costing me a dollar to boot!'

2AB's history lesson next day was the last period

before lunch. Brooke collected her guitar from the staff-room on the way to the lesson, and as she approached she could hear the usual chatter from the class. When she entered the room carrying the guitar case the noise ceased abruptly and all eyes watched her place the guitar beside her desk.

'Right, boys, history books open at page sixty-eight.' Murmurs of dissension mingled with the rustle of pages turning. Brooke looked towards Drew. 'Have you collected everyone's assignments?' she asked him.

'Yes, Miss Drynan.' He stood up and carried the pile of essay books out to her desk, his eyes drawn to the guitar case on the floor.

'I hope you haven't got a machine gun in that case, miss,' quipped Drew. 'You know, mow us all down if we don't pay attention.'

The boys were still laughing when he took his seat.

'Don't go putting ideas into my head, Drew Bastien,' Brooke intervened. 'No, that's just what it looks like, and today I'm going to prove to you all that you can enjoy history in a way that you haven't thought about before. Firstly, we're going to read through this chapter on the early history of the penal colony in New South Wales, and I'm going to keep the good bit until last.'

A sense of anticipation probably mixed with old-fashioned curiosity held the boys' attention while they worked through the set chapter in their textbooks. They seemed to have developed an interest in what Brooke was telling them, and by the time she lifted her guitar from its case she knew she had captured their attention and prepared to fire their imaginations.

She explained to them how ballads related to historical events and eras. Before and after each song they discussed the theme and to what section of their lesson the ballad referred.

The boys were enthralled. Halfway through the last song, which contained a simple repetitive chorus, Brooke had the class join in, the lunch bell sounded.

For the first time in the history of 2AB not a boy batted an eyelid or budged an inch. And when Brooke leant her guitar up against her desk they even clapped for more.

However, she dismissed the class, telling them she hoped she had given them a new interest in the dreaded subject, and turned to clear the blackboards while they all filed out to lunch. Dusting her hands, she went to collect her books together, only to find Drew standing looking longingly at her guitar.

'Can I carry your guitar back to the staffroom for you?' he asked a little selfconsciously.

'Of course. Thanks very much,' she smiled at him as she passed him the instrument to return to its case. 'Did you enjoy the lesson?' she couldn't help asking him.

'It was great. Really great,' he replied. 'You play pretty great, too, Brooke. Oh, sorry—Miss Drynan. Did it take you long to learn to play so well?' he asked seriously.

'Well, I can't really remember how long it took me to play fluidly. It seemed like ages at the time. I guess I had lessons for a few months or so and then it was simply a matter of practice.' She watched as he gently ran a finger over the strings.

'My mother used to play the guitar and I sort of have a go at playing hers. I've tried teaching myself, but it never seems to sound right somehow,' he sighed. 'Kley says my mother used to play for hours on end and that she was very good at it, too.'

'Have you tried to get hold of a book on how to play the guitar?' she asked.

He shook his head. 'No, I wouldn't know what to get.' He looked up at her enquiringly. 'Say, I don't suppose you could suggest one for me, could you, Brooke?'

'Better than that, I'll lend you a couple of mine.'

'Would you? That would be great. Can I walk home with you this afternoon and get them?' he asked eagerly.

'Well, I won't be heading off home until after four o'clock probably as we're having a teachers' meeting after classes.'

'Oh. And I have to go to swimming training, too.' He looked disappointed and then his face lit up again. 'Would you mind if I called around after dinner—I mean, if you're not going out or anything?'

'I think I'm free this evening,' she laughed. 'Bring your guitar with you and I'll give you a few pointers to start you off.'

So began Drew's twice-weekly guitar lessons. Surprisingly, he had a natural aptitude for the instrument and was soon playing quite well.

On one particular occasion Dave had accompanied Drew, and while the boy was practising a new set of chords in the living room Dave followed Brooke into the kitchenette where she was making them all a cup of tea. Dave relaxed against the breakfast bar, talking easily to Brooke about some work being done in his woodworking class.

The front door was wide open to catch the light evening breeze and none of them were aware of anyone's approach until the doorway was filled by a tall broad-shouldered frame and a dark head looked into the living room.

'Kley!' Drew exclaimed in surprise. 'What are you doing in town during the week?'

Both Dave and Brooke turned at the sound of the boy's voice.

'I wanted to see how you were getting on at school.' His voice was controlled, but his eyes moved across to Dave and Brooke, his expression making it plain what he thought of both Dave and Drew being there. 'Aunt Peg said you were down here.' This was almost an accusation.

Brooke felt guilty colour suffuse her face at the implications in his cold stare, but Dave wasn't perturbed in the slightest.

'Come on in, Kley,' he said, his voice a goodnatured welcome. 'You're just in time. Brooke's boiling the kettle. Tea or coffee?'

Brooke cringed inwardly, knowing what connotations Kley would be putting on Dave's easy familiarity.

Kley had stepped into the living room and walked easily towards the kitchen. 'Tea, thanks, if you're making it.' He looked levelly at Brooke.

'No trouble. Please sit down,' she said, and reached for another cup.

He sat down on a stool and Drew put down his guitar and brought the two extra chairs over to the breakfast bar. 'Did you have something to collect in town?' he asked his uncle, seating himself on the other stool beside Kley.

Dave set the boy's mug of coffee in front of him and sat down himself, leaving Brooke to bring Kley's cup with her own.

'No. As I said, I came to see how things were going with you at school. You've been back a couple of weeks now and as no one's been in touch with me regarding your misdemeanours, I became just a little suspicious.'

'Aw, Kley! Was I that bad?' Drew asked innocently, and his uncle gave him a dry look. 'Okay, Kley,' he grinned. 'But I'm a reformed character now.'

'And it's all Brooke's good work,' Dave laughed, putting his arm around Brooke's shoulders. 'Works wonders, this little lady. Not only is she beautiful but she's brainy.'

Kley's eyes moved deliberately from Dave's arm resting lightly on Brooke's shoulder to her face, and a cynical smile lifted the corners of his mouth. 'Obviously I've underestimated you, Brooke,' he said, and his double meaning was not lost on her. 'It appears I've been somewhat mistaken in my assessment of your,' he paused almost imperceptibly, 'abilities.'

'And Brooke's been giving me guitar lessons, too,' said Drew, while Dave looked sharply from Brooke to his friend. 'It's a pity you came tonight, Kley,' he continued, 'because I was going to surprise you when I thought I could play well enough, and now you know all about it.'

'Yes, it is a pity,' he said, and his eyes met Brooke's again over the rim of his teacup.

'Brooke brought her guitar to school for one of our history lessons and it was great fun.' Drew regaled his uncle while the three adults sat in silence, all aware of the underlying tensions in the room.

Eventually Kley looked at his watch. 'I suppose you should be getting home, Drew. School tomorrow.'

And Brooke sighed inwardly with relief. However, her relief was shortlived.

'Perhaps you could go along with Dave as I'd like to have a few words with Brooke before I follow you home.'

'Okay, Kley. I'll see you tomorrow, Brooke.' Drew looked at Dave, who seemed undecided about leaving, but he stood up at last and walked to the door with Drew.

'I'll see you tomorrow, too, Brooke,' he said quietly, and looked at Kley. 'See you later.'

'Yes. I won't be long.' Kley was giving his empty teacup his attention.

Brooke couldn't bring herself to look at him, waiting for the axe to fall, and her anger began to rise. He had no right to criticise her friendship with Dave! Nothing could be more innocent. If he was going to judge everyone by his own standards. . . .

'You appear to be getting along well with Drew,' he said.

'Thank you.' She looked at him in surprise, her anger slightly cooling at his lack of attack.

'However, if your interest has any ulterior motive behind it I suggest you start letting Drew down gently now. To give him a lot of attention and then forget about him when you tire of it will do him more harm than I think he can handle or you realise,' he said.

'Just what do you mean by that?' she demanded, standing facing him across the breakfast bar, her hands clutching the bench top.

'I think you know what I mean, Brooke,' he said evenly.

Because of her momentarily relaxed guard the barbs of his words found a deeper more vulnerable spot and the shock of pain reacted throughout her whole body. 'You are the most conceited. . . .' Her rash words to Jilly at Dave's party came back to her and she coloured guiltily, her anger turning back upon herself. 'I assure you I would never use a child as a pawn in any game,' she began. 'Surely you couldn't believe that of me?'

'Couldn't I?' he raised one arrogant eyebrow.

Her hand itched to slap his face again and one hand left the bench top.

'I wouldn't try it again, Brooke,' his hand closed painfully on her wrist, 'because next time I'll hit you back, believe me.'

Their eyes duelled in a battle of wills, neither one prepared to give an inch. Their anger burned the air between them, only to be joined by another less easily defined emotion. Who would have emerged the victor or whether the battle would have developed into something more potent would never be known because, at that precise moment, the click of heels on the front steps heralded Jilly's return home, and as she walked through the open door Kley reluctantly released Brooke's wrist and they both turned towards the other girl.

'Oh. Hi, there, you two! Long time since we saw you, Kley,' Jilly smiled, her eyes not missing Kley's tense stance and tightened jaw or the way Brooke was unconsciously rubbing the circulation back into her wrist.

Kley seemed to force himself to move. 'We've been tied up on the Downs, Jilly, but I hope to have more free time for a few weeks now.'

'Will you be staying in town?' asked Jilly, watching the other two with curiosity tinged with amusement.

'Just for a few days,' he replied, 'and I'd best be moving along, let you girls get to bed.' He moved towards the door. 'I'll be seeing you both. Thanks for the tea, Brooke.'

Jilly closed the door after him and turned back to watch Brooke as she cleared the used cups away and began washing them.

'Did you enjoy the play?' Brooke asked over-brightly.

'Mmmm. It wasn't bad.' Jilly watched her friend. 'Did you have an enjoyable evening?'

'Yes. Actually you just missed seeing Dave and Drew.'

'But I did get to see Kley,' laughed Jilly, 'although you didn't seem to be as impressed as I was by his visit.'

Brooke began wiping the crockery and didn't reply for a moment.

'He's the most overbearing, rude . . . oh! If I never see him again it will be too soon,' she finished.

'I see your relationship is coming along in leaps and bounds,' Jilly grinned as Brooke gave her a quelling look. 'I take it my dollar is still sitting pretty.' She ducked as Brooke threw the tea towel at her.

CHAPTER EIGHT

THE main topic under discussion at the teachers' meeting was the school excursions for the semester. Form teachers were to approach their respective classes and submit their proposals to the principal before final arrangements were made.

It was the policy of the school to have a day outing for each class at least once each semester. Brooke learned that tours were usually arranged to places of interest around the township. Previous excursions had been to the museum in the Old Stock Exchange, to the nearby seismic station as well as to numerous local businesses.

Brooke tackled 2AB about their prospective trip next morning. 'Now, how about a few realistic,' she emphasised, 'suggestions?' She looked hopefully at the class, expecting all sorts of outrageous destinations.

Instead of expressing enthusiasm at the idea of skipping a day in class the boys were looking a little uncomfortable, and for once no one seemed to want to comment.

'Well, what's the trouble? No one with an idea?' Brooke smiled. 'I find that hard to believe. I expected all kinds of impractical proposals, like a quick trip to the moon or some such.'

A couple of boys laughed halfheartedly.

'How about you, Drew? No thoughts on this?' she appealed to the class captain.

There was a short silence and then Drew stood up. 'Well, Miss Drynan, it's like this. We—that is, the first trip we had early in the year kind of went wrong and—er—I guess you could say we've been sort of grounded from any school outings.' He sat down slowly.

'Oh, I see.' Brooke glanced around and they all had the grace to look a little ashamed of themselves. 'Are you interested in going on a day trip or would you prefer to stay here at school?'

There were energetic cries in favour of the outing.

'We'd all like to have an outing, Miss Drynan, but the Boss was pretty adamant about our not having any more privileges for the rest of the year,' said Joey West unhappily.

'You were so badly behaved, hm?' Brooke's eyes ran over the boys and they all looked down at their desks. 'Well, it seems the trip's off,' she sighed.

There were disappointed cries of, 'Oh, miss!'

'Perhaps you could ask the Boss, Miss Drynan—you know, put in a good word for us,' suggested Drew. 'Maybe you could tell him we're reformed characters or something.' He looked at the other boys. 'We promise not to give you any hassles, honest.'

'Yeah! We promise, miss,' echoed the class.

'Perhaps I could,' replied Brooke thoughtfully.

The boys clapped and cheered loudly until she called for order.

'Good on you, miss,' said Joey West.

'I'll talk to Mr Mason, but you know I can't promise anything. If we sort out where you'd like to go I'll be able to present the whole idea to him. Any suggestions now?'

The way-out outweighed the sensible for a moment until Drew remarked that last term his uncle had offered to show the class over Terebori Downs. Of course, the principal had refused them permission to make the visit then, but he was sure that Kley would still be holding the offer open.

Although the boys lived in the middle of cattle country, the majority of them came from families who lived and worked in the city and rarely, if ever, had the opportunity to see a cattle station at close quarters. The children of the cattle families more often attended the other colleges as boarders. Only Drew and two of the other boys, whose fathers were stockmen, had any knowledge of the workings of a cattle property.

Brooke could see that they were all interested in the prospective visit to Terebori Downs where they would be able to see at first hand the daily management of a cattle station. According to Drew, Kley had offered earlier to show them a horse being broken, stockmen rounding up cattle, as well as the old goldmine on the property.

'Now, you're certain this visit will be all right with your uncle, Drew?'

'Sure, Miss Drynan,' he replied. 'Like I said, Kley suggested the whole thing last semester. Perhaps you could ring him if you'd like to check with him?'

Brooke's heart was beating agitatedly. She was sure Kley MacLean would be absolutely overjoyed to hear from her, and she took a deep breath to settle her nerves. 'All right, then, that's settled. Terebori Downs it is.'

She opened her notepad with fingers that weren't quite steady. 'I'll check with Drew's uncle tonight before I mention the visit to Mr Mason. If we go, we'll have to plan it all out. Firstly, we'll need a bus for transport. And then there'll be your lunch. I believe the money for the trips comes from class funds raised by the class at the semester fêtes. How much do 2AB have to hand, Drew?'

Once again the class shifted guiltily.

'I guess we don't have a cent, miss,' Drew replied slowly. 'We never got involved in the fêtes because we didn't get to go on the trips.'

'Oh!' Brooke's heart sank and there were murmurs throughout the room.

'Does that mean we can't go, miss?' asked Joey West.

'Well, we have to finance the trip with something. I don't think the school would be prepared to fund us. Perhaps one of the other classes could help,' she suggested.

The boys looked sceptical.

'What if we all put in some of our pocket money?' offered an Andrews twin.

'I don't know that that would be enough. I'll have to find out the cost of hiring a bus, for starters,' she told them. 'Anyway, we'll leave all that until I speak to Mr MacLean and Mr Mason, then we can take it from there. Now, back to *Macbeth*.'

That evening Brooke put a call through to Kley Mac-Lean at Aunt Peg's. He had said he would be in town for a few days, so she decided to try to reach him there first, before she allowed herself to even think about making the call. Aunt Peg told her that Kley had returned to the Downs that afternoon, and Brooke replaced the receiver.

'Now why would Brooke Drynan, who professes to dislike Kley MacLean intensely, want to be phoning him?' teased Jilly, coming into the living room fresh from her shower.

'Don't worry, Jilly. It's strictly business, believe me,' Brooke told her.

Jilly laughed and settled down in a beanbag chair with a magazine.

Brooke lifted the receiver again, a flutter in the pit of her stomach. For heaven's sake, why was she getting so uptight about what was to be purely a business call? If it wasn't for the boys she wouldn't be ringing him at all. She hardly knew the man, when all was said and done, and since that disconcerting moment overlooking the Burdekin River she had only set eyes on him once. After that encounter, which left her emotionally and physically bruised, she could see no reason to change her disparaging opinion of him.

Since that scene the evening before Brooke had been plunged to the very depths of depression. The incident on the riverbank had seemed so far apart from reality that she could almost convince herself that it had been nothing more than a figment of her imaginationn. When

Kley had reappeared the whole disturbing episode had returned with vivid intensity. Not only did he think she was trying to keep Dave and his wife apart, but now he had decided she was using Drew to get to him.

Each encounter with him had been purely physical, and if Jilly hadn't returned home when she did Brooke wondered where their animosity would have led them. She glanced at her wrist reflectively, at the faint bruise which remained to indicate the place where his fingers had held her in a vice-like grip. Her heart began to hammer in her breast and the flutter in the pit of her stomach returned. She could almost feel the painful grasp of his strong fingers.

With a sigh of exasperation she determinedly dialled the number of Terebori Downs, glancing at her wrist-watch as she listened to the ring at the other end. It was seven-thirty, so he should be home.

When a strange voice answered her call her heart jumped into her mouth. No, it certainly wasn't deep enough to be Kley.

'May I speak to Kley MacLean, please?' Her voice had risen a tone higher than normal as she tried to quell her nervousness.

'Kley? Sorry, lassie. He went down to look at one of the mares who's due to foal. This is Dougal Mac-Pherson, can I help you instead?'

'I'm Drew's form teacher, Brooke Drynan, and I'd like to discuss our class outing with Mr MacLean. I believe he offered to show the class over Tere-bori Downs last semester. Perhaps you could ask him to phone me when he comes in, if you wouldn't mind?'

'Surely, lassie,' the accented voice replied. 'He shouldn't be long unless old Tessa decides to produce her offspring tonight.'

Well, that was that. She replaced the receiver and picked up her library book, joining Jilly in the living-room. She had turned three pages before she realised she hadn't taken in a single word of the plot as she kept glancing over at the telephone waiting for it to ring. Jilly's knowing smile brought an expression of self-disgust to Brooke's face and she sprang out of her chair, deciding to take a shower and wash her hair.

She lingered under the soothing tepid spray for longer than was necessary and leisurely towelled herself dry. Wrapping her terry towelling bathrobe about her, she began to give her wet hair a vigorous drying rub.

The telephone jangled as she walked into the bedroom, and before she could move she could hear Jilly speaking. It had to be Kley. She moved slowly into the living-room, and judging by the beaming smile on Jilly's face it couldn't be anyone else.

'Here she is now, Kley. She was in the shower,' Jilly was saying. His reply had her laughing heartily. 'Sorry to disappoint you on that score.' Jilly's eyes rested on Brooke's bathrobe, leaving Brooke to make what she liked of the one-sided conversation.

Jilly handed the phone to Brooke with her usual audacious wink.

'Hello, Kley. Brooke here.' Her voice was sharper than usual.

'Sorry I wasn't here when you rang earlier,' he said. 'Dougal mentioned something about Drew. He hasn't been up to his old tricks, has he?'

'No, of course not.' She leapt to the boy's defence as she recognised a note of 'I wondered how long it would be before the rot set in' in his voice. Or perhaps it was herself she was defending. She explained succinctly about their outing and asked him if he was still prepared to have the boys for the day.

'Yes, of course,' he said, after a short pause, 'if you're sure you want to bring the little tearaways.'

'They won't be any trouble,' she began indignantly, and he laughed softly.

'What day do you want to bring the boys out here?'

Reluctantly Brooke explained the position, how she had to get permission for the boys to go as well as arranging their transportation on a shoestring because of their limited funds.

There was another short silence. 'I see. Against all odds. You'd better leave it to me, Brooke. I'll see what I can do and phone you tomorrow evening. If we can swing it, it should prove to be an interesting day,' he remarked drily.

'Yes.' Brooke wondered just what he meant by that. 'Well, I'll let you get back to your horse.'

'Oh, Tessa's fine. It's her third foal, so she's taking it in her stride, no pun intended,' he laughed, and her pulses leaped alarmingly.

'Mmmm,' she replied without humour, which caused another low rumble of mirth to vibrate along the wires.

When he rang off Brooke stood looking at the receiver as it buzzed in her hand, a frown of irritation on her face.

'What's he done now?' asked Jilly, passing Brooke a cup of coffee.

'Taken over,' replied Brooke tersely. 'I'm to leave it all to him to arrange. He has the most nerve of anyone I've ever met! If it wasn't for the boys' benefit I'd be inclined to tell him where to take his Terebori Downs and every one of his overbearing ancestors!'

Jilly was highly amused. 'You should learn to let men do it all, Brooke, instead of being so independent. It panders to their male egos if they can play the big guide and protector. Now you won't have to go running around yourself. Just sit back and enjoy it.'

'If Dave or anyone else offered it wouldn't worry me,' said Brooke. 'It's just that man is so . . . so high-handed. Oh, I can't explain it, Jilly. He just rubs me up the wrong way.'

The other girl looked at Brooke thoughtfully. 'Have

you ever stopped to wonder why he ruffles your feathers?'

'Why? Because I can't stand conceit, arrogance, egoism. . . .'

'I get the picture, Brooke,' laughed Jilly. 'But I think the lady doth protest too much somehow.'

'Protest about what?' Brooke looked sharply at her friend.

'About disliking Kley. I don't think either of you dislikes each other as much as you say you do. In fact, I don't think you dislike each other at all.' Jilly nodded at Brooke's shocked face.

'Your imagination never fails to amaze me, Jilly Martin,' exclaimed Brooke. 'You couldn't be more wrong.'

'We'll see,' said Jilly knowingly.

Two days later everything had been arranged with the minimum of effort on Brooke's part and no fuss whatsoever. Kley MacLean had taken care of it all.

The owner of the local bus service was a friend of Kley's and he was supplying a bus to take the boys out to the Downs free of charge. A barbecue lunch would be provided and the meat, salad and bread rolls were also being kindly supplied by some more friends of Kley's. When Brooke queried him regarding the cooking of steaks for over thirty boys Kley had waved her question airily aside, remarking grandly that Dougal could cook for thirty or three hundred at Terebori Downs. He had also suggested that they bring their swimming trunks so that they could have a cooling swim in the creek before they left for home.

However, if she grudgingly admired his diligent organisation, one part of the whole thing grated on her nerves like chalk squeaking on a blackboard. He had even had the audacity to contact the principal before Brooke had had time to approach him herself to put forward her case. As far as John Mason was concerned, he was quite happy to allow the boys to visit the Downs as Kley's guests, and the outing had been already arranged between the two men for the following Tuesday.

All that was left for Brooke to do was to thank the principal and Kley MacLean on behalf of the boys and to organise things her end.

Just once, she begged anyone in the hot blue sky who cared to listen, just once let me be around to see that paragon of male chauvinism come a cropper. Just once!

CHAPTER NINE

THE bus turned off the bitumen road at the rough weathered signpost that read 'Terebori Downs' and rattled along an unsealed section for some half mile or so before reaching the large white gate in the fence marking the boundary of the cattle station. The fences were tidily symmetrical and well tended, seemingly running off to infinity to both the left and right of the track, and sturdy wooden posts on either side of the gate supported the station's name plate, also gleaming white.

'Terebori Downs' was printed evenly across the top, etched into the board, and underneath, in equally bold letters, 'MacLean'. Not Kley MacLean, just simply 'MacLean'.

One of the boys had swung open the gate and the bus protested in every join as it vibrated across the cattle grid. The gate firmly latched behind them, they proceeded on their way, across MacLean land. Brooke experienced a surge of excitement that they were almost there at last.

The boys seemed to share her feelings, judging by the increased volume of their chatter, until Dave demanded that they keep it down to a dull roar. Dave's presence had been a last-minute stipulation by the principal to assist Brooke in organising the class for the day.

The countryside through which they passed, although appearing rather dry and desolate to some, still retained an air of prosperity. Clumps of stunted trees dotted the area and there was an abundance of dry waving grass. Here and there small outcrops of weathered rocks formed small hillocks, dotting the landscape, and healthy cattle, all steers, Brooke noticed, roamed freely. For all their existence in this dry and barren outback country the animals were far from thin and undernourished, but to Brooke's admittedly unpractised eye they looked sleek and contented, raising their heads in bored indifference as the bus ambled across the plain, leaving a trail of dust in its wake.

Some fifteen minutes later the bus driver changed down a gear as the road began to climb to the top of a slight incline. Here the shrubs were taller and grew thicker, and with a spurt of renewed excitement Brooke wondered if this was the same rise that the first Mac-Lean family had climbed all those years ago.

Before them lay Terebori Downs homestead, nestling on a gently rising hill amid tall shady trees. At least the trees surrounding the house were taller than the natural shrubs covering the land through which they had been travelling.

Whitewashed walls and a shining galvanised iron roof shimmered in the intensifying sunlight, giving all the impressions of being a mirage, an oasis in the desert. The abundance of greener growth to the right of the homestead was obviously the spring and its gently flowing stream Kley had spoken about. The course of the creek seemed to disappear behind another of the undulating hills. The whole scene was one of peace and tranquillity.

The bus grumbled to a halt in front of the wide verandah of the homestead. Verandahs completely surrounded the house, with the overhanging roof providing welcome shade from the relentless sun.

Although Brooke had been looking forward to her first glimpse of the homestead she found her eyes were drawn immediately to the tall suntanned figure standing at the top of the wide steps leading up on to the verandah. Inexplicably her breath caught in her throat as her eyes moved to him, no less compellingly attractive than she remembered and her sleepless nights had painted him. He leant easily against the verandah post, one brown hand resting on the post and the other hooked into the wide low-slung belt of his faded blue denims. A pale blue and white checked shirt strained across his muscular chest and shoulders, the sleeves rolled up to expose strong arms glistening bronze in the sunlight.

His smile welcomed the boys as they began to file out of the bus. Dave climbed down with the first few boys and hailed Kley goodnaturedly from the bottom of the steps. The other man's expression scarcely changed, but still Brooke was reluctant to leave the sanctuary of the bus. Then the last boy filed out and she had to make a move. As she went to alight he was there to take her hand to help her down the steps on to the dusty ground before Dave could turn around.

'Welcome to Terebori Downs, Miss Drynan,' his voice was lowly smooth while his cynical smile wasn't masked in his eyes as they crinkled up against the glare.

'Come and meet Dougal, Miss Drynan,' called Drew from the verandah.

For the first time Brooke noticed the short wizened little man standing beside Drew.

'Move up on to the verandah, boys.' Kley made a path for her through the throng of 2AB's. 'Cool drinks are ready on the table over there.' He turned to Brooke. 'This is Dougal, Brooke, who sees to our home comforts. Dougal, meet Drew's teacher, Brooke Drynan.'

'Pleased to meet you. I've heard a lot about you, lassie, from young Andrew.' The old man's Scottish brogue enchanted Brooke, although just what age the old-timer was she couldn't hazard a guess. His hair was almost white and his face weathered by the sun and heat, but his bright blue eyes twinkled alertly and his step was spritely in spite of his limp, which Drew had said he sustained breaking a horse.

The boys trooped after Dougal to the trestle table where paper cups were filled with welcome cool drinks. Drew handed one to Brooke and she thankfully relieved her dry throat.

'Dave can stay and supervise the boys while they quench their thirsts. Come in and I'll show you the homestead.' Kley took her elbow, leading her through what was obviously the main set of double doors. Looking along the length of the verandah it seemed that all rooms had openings on to the verandah via sets of double doors.

'This is the living-room and incorporates the only remaining section of the old homestead, along with part of the kitchen which backs on to this.'

He stood in the centre of what was clearly a much used section of the MacLean home. It was a lived-in room with a clean worn carpet square on a highly polished wooden floor, with large comfortable-looking chairs. A neat pile of magazines sat on a solid coffee table and what was surely a major part of Drew's shell collection rested on the sideboard.

Half a dozen framed photographs caught Brooke's eye, and she walked curiously across to have a closer look at a studio portrait of the two MacLean children taken when Kley was around about Drew's age. The young girl in the photo was very much like Kley, although the feminine planes of her face were much softer, giving the promise of youthful beauty. As for Kley, the strength was still there even at that young age, but his eyes, minus the cool cynicism that she always saw in their blue depths, were gay and full of life as Drew's often were.

She looked up to find those same eyes on her and smiled selfconsciously. 'You haven't changed much.'

'I'm most flattered,' he nodded unsmilingly with a slight trace of derision, 'considering that the photo was taken nearly twenty years ago.'

A huge rough stone fireplace dominated one corner of the room and Kley told her that this had been built by James MacLean in the first homestead, the fireplace and the rough brick wall between the living-room and the kitchen.

Dougal's kitchen was neat and spotless and had recently been remodelled, gleaming cupboards and bench tops blending in without detracting from what remained of the past. This included the largest scrubbed wooden table Brooke had ever seen, and although a modern new range was in evidence, the large old fireplace and hearth bore signs of still being in use.

A door led off the kitchen into a large pantry which Kley told her was used as their cold store before the days of refrigeration. Walking inside, Brooke was surprised at the drop in temperature.

Kley held the screen door open for her to precede him out on to the back verandah and the waves of heat broke over them as they stood there, bringing home to Brooke just how cool it had been in the brick-walled pantry.

Dougal was obviously a busy and successful gardener. One fenced-off section contained a thriving vegetable patch while to the right was a chicken coop with healthy chickens scratching in the dusty grass. Their spring, Kley said, was worth its weight in gold to them as they could pump the water up from the creek to keep the vegetable garden irrigated.

From where she stood on the verandah Brooke was able to see the extent of the station proper. There were numerous buildings besides the homestead, one huge galvanised iron shed housing machinery of every imaginable description, while a group of smaller cottages were apparently quarters for the stockmen and their families.

Everywhere one looked there were wooden fences containing horses or cattle or tidy buildings. In fact, Terebori Downs gave all the appearance of being a small settlement, almost a township in itself.

'I wasn't aware that Dave was coming along today?' Kley's question was all but a rebuke as his eyes surveyed his domain.

'It was John Mason's idea,' she said defensively. 'He

decided at the last minute that Dave should come with us.'

'Didn't he think you could handle the boys alone?' he asked disdainfully.

'I've been handling the boys alone since the beginning of the semester, Mr MacLean.' Her colour rose with her temper. 'Dave's presence was meant to be a helping hand, not a vote of incompetence.'

He looked blandly at her for a few moments. 'When I was speaking to Dave last week he said things were going very well between him and Jacqui. I'd rather like it to stay that way.'

'You're beginning to sound like a broken record, and I'm finding it exceptionally boring.' The words came out through Brooke's teeth and she noticed his jaw tighten. They seemed to have started the day on a brilliant note. She sighed exasperatedly. 'As hard as it may be for you to believe this,' she said sarcastically, 'I'm in full agreement with you in that respect.'

He was looking at her sceptically.

'I don't know why I'm even bothering to explain, but Dave and I are just good friends, nothing more, nothing less,' she told him firmly.

Kley went to pass a comment, and judging by his expression, not a peacemaking one, as Drew loped along the hallway in search of them.

'Hey, come on, you two! We're all raring to go out here. The fellows don't want to waste a single minute,' he grinned.

His uncle nodded. 'We're on our way.' He motioned Brooke before him through the doorway.

'Where are we going first, Mr MacLean? Can we watch you ride a bucking bronco?' asked Joey West.

'I'd like to have a go at that. That'd be neat,' beamed a freckle-faced Andrews twin.

'I think we'll leave that until rodeo time,' said Kley, and grinned at the disappointed murmurs. 'We'll see what we can do. First up,' he continued, 'we'll take a

look over the home base workings before it gets too
hot. I'll explain how we go about running the Downs as
we walk along. Everyone ready?'

'What were you and Kley talking about before that
kept you out the back for so long?' Dave asked Brooke
as he joined her at the tail of the group.

'Nothing much,' she said, looking at him quickly and
catching a teasing twinkle in his eyes. 'Not you too,
Dave. I couldn't stand it. I have enough of that from
Jilly.'

'Whatever do you mean, Brooke?' he grinned. 'I
thought you'd find Kley attractive. Most girls do.'

'I'm not most girls,' she all but snapped, 'and
anyway, we weren't out the back all that long.'

'You didn't look overly pleased when you rejoined
us,' Dave prompted.

'I'm afraid your friend has the uncanny knack of
knowing how to raise my temper and my blood pressure,' she replied, her eyes fixed on a spot between
Kley's broad shoulders.

'What did he say?' Dave put a friendly hand on her
shoulder as they walked along.

'Well, if you must know, he remarked on the possi-
bility that you were along today because I might not be
able to handle the boys.'

'Was that all?'

'Isn't that enough?' Brooke appealed, and sighed. 'He
also warned me not to give you any encouragement
romantically.'

Dave laughed spontaneously, drawing Kley's attention to them, and Brooke's eyes fell to the dusty track
rather than meet his steely gaze.

'Now I wonder why he'd do that?' mused Dave
softly, almost to himself.

With Kley leading they walked for what seemed like
kilometres all over the home area, and as they moved
from one section to another Kley kept them enthralled
with stories of life on the Downs in present and bygone
days.

'My great-great-grandfather encountered a lot of problems when he set up his home in the virtually un-explored outback,' he told them. 'They built rough yards out of saplings to hold the cattle and they would take their herd out to graze each day until the herd grew accustomed to the new grazing ground. There were no fences to keep them together, so they had trouble keeping track of their cattle. Every so often the stockmen would go out "gulley raking", that is, collecting the cattle living and breeding in the valleys or gulleys. Then the cleanskins or unmarked animals were branded and counted.'

'What about cattle rustlers, Mr MacLean? Did they have them, too?' asked Joey West.

'Yes, the cattle duffers often drove off large numbers to mountain hideouts where their brands were changed before they were sold,' replied Kley with amusement.

They passed one corral where a bright evil eye gazed at them through the rails. This was Kley's stud bull, and only the very daring approached his pen.

Surprisingly the boys were interested in Kley's experiments with pasture improvements. In place of the spear grass he was introducing Townsville lucerne which was developed from a plant accidentally introduced from South America, and he explained that this factor, along with regular fertilisation, was giving the Downs a tre-mendous increase in beef production. Shorthorn cattle reared on native pasture reached slaughter weight in five or six years, whereas those raised on Townsville lucerne reached the same weight in less than three years. The crop also enabled cattlemen to run more beasts per acre.

'Knowledgeable, isn't he?' teased Dave as the three of them walked together towards the next section of their tour. 'Bet you thought he was just a pretty face, didn't you, Brooke?'

She raised her eyebrows and Kley laughed.

'Oh, Brooke knows I'm more than a pretty face,' he said, smilingly sure of himself, as he marched on ahead of them leaving Brooke's face pink in the sweltering sun.

They had moved on to the horses and Kley introduced them to Vengeance, the horse Drew had told Brooke about that day on Magnetic Island. He was a magnificent beast, who threw up his head when the boys approached only to nuzzle Kley's hand for a cube of sugar.

'Can we see the new foal?' asked Drew.

'Oh, has Tessa had her foal?' Brooke turned to Kley.

'Two days ago,' he told her. 'A colt. It's our first sired by Vengeance and he's a beauty.'

The little foal, all long slender legs, pressed close to his mother as the boys took turns to peep into the stall. While Brooke looked on Kley went into the stall and patted the mare.

'How are you, old girl?' The mare turned to nuzzle Kley and turned contentedly back to her foal.

Brooke was smiling at the foal when Kley turned back to her. 'Isn't he cute, Kley? He has such soft brown eyes that you feel like giving him a hug.'

'I've got soft brown eyes,' said Dave behind her. 'How about a hug for me?'

At Brooke's half amused, half exasperated expression he laughed softly and moved away to check on a couple of boys who had begun to climb over a corral fence.

Brooke's eyes moved to Kley and she felt her colour rise, and she was unable to drag her eyes from his. His smile faded, his eyelashes masking his eyes. The air between them seemed to crackle until Brooke felt she could bear it no longer. In fact Kley was moving towards her when Joey West's voice broke the spell.

'Now can we watch you breaking a horse, Mr Mac-Lean?'

Kley blinked slowly, the tension in the set of his jaw faded. 'We'll go over to the corral now, Joey, but I'm just going to make up the audience today. My head stockman, Archie Kerwin, has been working with this particular horse, so he'll be doing all the riding.' He gave Tessa one more pat before they set off across the paddock.

Keeping her eyes to the ground, Brooke felt her knees turn weak as she recalled that moment of undeniable attraction which had sprung unbidden between them in the stable. Had they been alone she knew he would have taken her in his arms, his intention had been in the intensity of his blue gaze, in the throb of the pulse in his jaw. And she had a disturbing feeling that she wouldn't have been able to raise one shred of resistance.

On reaching the corral they followed Kley's example by climbing on to the bottom rung of the fence and leaning over the top. An attractive-looking piebald was tethered to the fence on the opposite side of the yard. It danced about a little, tossing its head and rolling its eyes at the sudden audience. The boys talked excitedly until Kley asked them to watch quietly so as not to upset the animal.

An Aboriginal stockman, wearing the usual tight-legged denims, bright checked shirt and high-heeled riding boots, came ambling towards them. He tipped his well worn hat to the back of his head and a shy smile creased his dark face.

'Morning, boss. You want to try old Smoky here?'

Kley returned his greeting. 'No, Arch, the boys want to see an expert on the job. How about it?'

'No worries, boss. He's just about ready.' Archie moved off with a typical rolling gait, calling to another young stockman to bring a saddle.

'When Archie climbs on the horse I want you all to jump back from the fence if he bucks this way. We don't want any accidents,' Kley told them.

'What does breaking a horse involve, Mr MacLean? Do you just throw a saddle on the horse and jump on, like in the movies?' asked one of the boys.

'Not exactly. It takes lots of work and patience,' Kley replied. 'Once in the breaking yard we rope the horse and tie him to a post. And after a while he realises he can't pull away. Most good stockmen can soothe a horse simply by talking quietly to it. Archie over there has that knack, that's why he's good at his job.

'Before fitting the horse with a bridle to harden its mouth Arch gets the horse used to a rope halter. For the past couple of days he's had the saddle on the horse and had been teaching it to respond to the reins without actually climbing into the saddle.'

The piebald snorted warningly as Archie approached, murmuring reassuringly. Quickly and deftly he had the animal saddled and, in a flash, taking both the horse and the audience by surprise, he vaulted on to the horse's back.

The piebald spun around in indignation, trying to unseat the unaccustomed weight. Archie clung to the animal as though he was moulded to it and his wide white grin mirrored his enjoyment. After a short time he drew in the reins, bringing the piebald's head up close to its body, preventing it from bucking, and soon the horse was trotting around the yard. Archie slid to the ground still holding the horse firmly, patting its neck, talking soothingly, until he motioned the other young stockman to come and lead the horse away.

The boys gave Archie a clap and he swept off his hat in a mock bow. He discussed the horse with Kley for a few moments and then disappeared after the other man and the horse.

A large open-backed truck rumbled around the corner of the stable and pulled up amid a cloying cloak of dust. Kley directed the boys to climb aboard for a lift back to the homestead.

'You'd better sit in the cabin,' suggested Kley, holding the door open for Brooke to slide in beside the driver, a nice-looking young man who was more than pleased to have her beside him. He kept up light conversation all the way back to the homestead.

Kley had stepped up on to the running board where

he could keep an eye on Dave and the boys in the back, and Brooke couldn't tell whether or not he could hear their conversation over the roar of the engine. The next thing he'd be telling her not to encourage his men, she thought wryly, disturbingly aware of the brown arm wrapped around the window of the truck, muscles flexed as he balanced on the jolting vehicle.

At the homestead they loaded the food and Dougal on to the truck and headed down to the creek where they decided to look over the old goldmine while Dougal and Sam, the driver of the truck, along with the bus driver, who had nominated himself as kitchen hand, made the preparations for lunch, stoking up the huge barbecue plate and setting the steaks on to sizzle. Brooke offered to stay and help, but Dougal firmly declined her offer, telling her, his blue eyes twinkling, that he'd not be denying her the scramble up the hill to see such an interesting sight.

And so they set off, hats planted firmly on heads, taking the rough track in single file. Kley and Dave picked out the easiest route, and yet by the time they had reached the relatively flat area before the mine they were hot and sticky and out of breath. Talking excitedly, the boys gathered around the mine entrance, a hole about three and a half feet wide and five feet high, that had been dug into the crumbling rock face of the hill. The harder stone still bore the scores of the bite of the pick, although the timber around the shaft looked quite new. Kley explained that he had had the old timber replaced for safety's sake.

The boys were clamouring to go into the mine shaft, so Kley quickly had them divided into small groups of five or six, ready to venture inside in turn. He disappeared into the entrance for a moment and returned with an old kerosene lantern which he lit, adjusting the flame.

Not looking forward to going into the dark crevice, Brooke waited until only four boys and herself were left.

'Don't get lost in there,' called Dave, and Brooke shivered as she took a deep breath and followed the others into the shaft of darkness, ducking her head for the first ten feet or so as the roof of the tunnel was only about five feet high. However, once they were inside the actual cavity where Andrew MacLean had extracted his gold, the roof rose to about a foot above Kley's head and was roughly twelve feet long and eight feet wide.

The lantern only illuminated part of the underground room, and as Kley moved about the light flickered eerily, and it wasn't solely due to the much cooler air that caused Brooke to have to suppress an urge to dive for the entrance.

Kley was explaining that Andrew would use his pick and shovel to loosen the earth and load it on to a small trolley to truck it out into the sunlight. The trolley had run on rails, but these had long since disappeared. Once outside Andrew washed the stony soil to separate the gold by diverting a channel of running water from the spring. The mine had only been moderately successful and barely worth Andrew's efforts.

'Wow, isn't it scarey in here?' remarked an Andrews twin with obvious relish. 'If the opening caved in we could be lost in here for ever.'

'Yeah! We'd all choke without any air,' said one of the other boys, making a very good imitation of someone doing just that.

Brooke looked towards the opening of light, which seemed all of a sudden so far away, and she turned cold all over, her mouth dry with rising panic. She had never felt comfortable in confined spaces, but this was a hundred times worse.

She must have made some sound as she started to move towards the light and the blessed openness beyond, because a strong hand took hold of her elbow in the dimness as she stumbled on the rock-strewn floor.

'Watch your step, Miss Drynan,' the even timbre of his tone steadying her rising hysteria. 'We'll rejoin the others now. Lead the way, young Andrews. Off you go, and mind your heads.' His hand remained firmly on her arm until they reached the opening.

The glare after the semi-darkness was so blinding it was almost painful. Brooke took a deep breath of relief and turned to thank Kley for helping her to keep her cool, but he was already organising the boys for the downhill trek and wasn't even looking in her direction. She sighed resentfully, imagining what he was thinking. Scared of the dark on top of everything else. Another point in her disfavour.

Dougal's steaks were sizzling deliciously on the huge barbecue plate by the time they had scrambled back to the camp and the boys were more than ready to do justice to their lunch. They lined up for their rolls and salad, and when Dougal added the steak to their burgers they sat around in the shade of the trees suddenly weary from their energetic morning.

While Dave was serving the last of the boys Brooke found a very comfortable log in a patch of shade and she had no sooner settled when Kley joined her. She bit enthusiastically into her burger, determined not to allow him to upset her lunch, only to have the sauce run through her fingers. Kley raised an eyebrow in amusement as she tried to save the droplets with her tongue. Then he was wiping her chin with his handkerchief, the touch of his fingers bringing hot colour to her cheeks, but he had turned away again, his attention intent upon his own burger.

'I'm sorry I made a fool of myself in the mine,' she found herself saying. 'I'm not much in confined spaces, I'm afraid, so I shouldn't have gone inside.'

'Not if you suffer from claustrophobia,' he agreed.

'I wouldn't say I suffer from claustrophobia,' she began, perversely annoyed by his agreeableness.

'You just don't like confined spaces,' he finished,

amusement in his voice. 'Come now, admit your Achilles' heel, Brooke. We all have one.'

'And what's your Achilles' heel, Mr MacLean?' Brooke seethed.

'Now that's a closely guarded secret, Miss Drynan,' he laughed. He had turned his eyes lazily to her face in that boldly intimate way of his. 'But it could be a very interesting exercise for you to try to uncover it. For both of us.' His eyes danced teasingly.

'I'm just as sure it would be a waste of time and energy,' she replied between her teeth.

'Oh, I don't know,' he goaded.

'Room for one more on your log?' Dave sat down on the other side of Brooke. 'Don't let me interrupt your conversation,' he added, looking from Brooke's set expression to Kley's wry amusement. 'You two crossing verbal swords again? That should make for a very entertaining lunch.'

Brooke kept her eyes on her burger, but Kley must have given Dave an intimidating look, for Dave chuckled. 'Sorry. I will tease on the odd occasion.' And the conversation turned to less provoking general topics.

Their lunch taken care of, while they waited the recommended time after eating before going swimming, Kley sat with the boys regaling them with stories of station life and answering their many questions. Brooke and Dave helped Dougal clear away their luncheon debris.

The boys wore their swimming trunks beneath their jeans and they had all made a dash for the cooling water of the creek before the grown-ups could turn around.

'You coming in for a swim, Kley?' asked Dave, struggling out of his shirt.

'Sure am,' Kley replied as he pulled open the press studs on the front of his own shirt, baring his firm brown chest.

Like a magnet Brooke's eyes were drawn to his body, her breath a constriction in her throat. When his brown fingers unbuckled the belt of his jeans she dragged her gaze from him and began to move quickly towards the water's edge. 'I ... I'll keep an eye on the boys,' she said as she moved away.

'Aren't you coming in for a swim?' Kley asked from behind her. He had caught up with her and she shook her head, keeping her eyes averted from his near naked body.

'Chicken!' he chuckled softly as he passed her and dived into the cool depths of the pool, with Dave close on his tail, although Dave didn't enter the water with the sharp precision of his friend.

Dougal joined her on the creek bank and they watched the antics of the boys in the water. Brooke watched the pool with a kind of fascination, waiting for a strong muscular body to break the surface, and she was glad when three o'clock arrived and she could call them out of the water for afternoon tea which Dougal had prepared.

He had cooked damper, a mixture of plain wheat flour and water, kneaded into a flat cake, in the coals of the fire, and it was delicious eaten with cups of true billy tea.

All too soon they had dressed and were in the truck heading the short distance to the homestead. The bus was parked in the shade of the trees and the driver soon had it pulled up in front of the verandah ready to load up for their return journey.

Joey West was deputised to thank Kley and Dougal on behalf of the class and Dave began to organise the reluctant file of boys on to the bus. Brooke added her thanks to the boys' as she balanced on the bottom step of the bus. Taking her outstretched hand in his, he assured her that the day had been his pleasure and, releasing her hand, he lowered one eyelid swiftly in a wink, leaving her to make what she liked of that.

Next morning the class was still talking enthusiastically about their visit to Terebori Downs. Even the knowledge that they were to write up an account of their excursion didn't dim their excitement.

Drew thanked Brooke for arranging the outing and for what he called 'soft soaping' the principal, and then he informed her that, for the first time, the class had decided to join in the activities associated with the fête. They had decided to put on a thirty-minute play-cum-concert as their contribution to the day and they would like the permission of the principal to use the form room directly beneath their home room. It was on ground level and they had discovered that it would be free on the day of the fête.

The High School fêtes always featured special displays arranged by each class. A nominal entry fee was charged for each display and the money raised financed breaking up day celebrations and, on very successful occasions, donations by the classes were made to the school library or sporting facilities.

Rather dubiously Brooke enquired about the nature of the concert they planned, much to the amusement of the boys.

'Did you think we were planning a bit of a wild disco, miss?' laughed Joey West, 'with us all decked out in iridescent suits plus a couple of strippers to finish off for good measure. Say, that wouldn't be a bad idea,' he teased.

When the laughter died away Drew hastened to reassure her,

'Actually, you gave us the idea, Miss Drynan. We're going to do the story about the discovery of gold and we thought we'd use old folk songs to tell the story, like you did in our history lesson last week. We've got a band together, an old country style band. Jeff's father has made him a bass out of an old tea chest, Pete's on the wooden scrubbing board, Don's on harmonica, Jim's blowing on an old wine flagon and I'm on guitar.'

'We're all involved, miss,' added Joey. 'Some of us are singing, others are working on the sets in wood-working class and old Dan over there, who's totally tone-deaf, is collecting the money.'

'What do you think, Miss Drynan? We got together last weekend and wrote it all down and the fellows thought maybe you could read it over and see if you think it's okay,' finished Drew.

And that was what Brooke did during her lunch break, much to the surprise of her colleagues.

'What's that you've got your nose in, Brooke?' asked Peter Malpass, who walked into the staffroom with his wife.

'2AB's idea for their activity at the fête,' she replied absently, so that she missed the disbelieving looks and shaken heads of her fellow teachers.

She was astounded that the class could come up with something so polished. The story was simple but well illustrated by the chosen songs, most of which she re-cognised as coming from a collection of folk songs she had loaned Drew when he started playing the guitar.

The boys worked feverishly at their plans, using free activities periods as well as time before and after school, and as the day of the fête drew nearer Brooke was amazed and definitely proud of their efforts. She took great delight in informing her colleagues of their progress, as most of the other teachers were still sceptical about 2AB's apparent change of behavioural pattern. They had been astonished that the day trip to Terebori Downs had been accomplished without incident, and Brooke had to stop herself from showing a decided smugness.

And all their efforts paid off, as their display was a huge success. Because of the large number of people wanting to see it the boys had had to do a second show. Now they were finishing up the clearing away of sets, etc.

'Miss Drynan,' Drew's voice turned Brooke back to face the boys who had all clustered around their form captain. He cleared his throat exaggeratedly. 'Miss Drynan, we, the terrors of the school, now known as the lambs. . . .'

'Angels,' said someone at the back, and they all laughed.

'Now known as the angelic lambs,' continued Drew, 'have all chipped in to show our appreciation of your help and efforts in this our very successful project, and we would like you to accept this small gift with our thanks.' He brought his hand from behind his back and placed a square parcel in Brooke's hands.

It was wrapped in pale blue paper and sported an elaborate floppy red bow on the top. Brooke looked at the boys and slowly untied the ribbon and removed the wrapping. The box felt heavy and she shook it slightly, glancing suspiciously at the faces gathered around her.

'Open it, miss—go on!'

'It's not alive, is it?' she asked them, and they laughed merrily, denying it fervently. 'I mean, it's not another toad or a spider?' They shook their heads and promised faithfully that it wasn't.

Gingerly she lifted the lid. In a bed of pale blue tissue lay a nicely shaped glass, the lip edged with gold. Brooke lifted it out of the box, a curious lump in her throat. On one side was the gilded seal of the city and on the other side was the slogan 'Charters Towers— City of Gold'.

She was overcome. 'Boys, thank you very much. It's really beautiful, and I'll treasure it.'

They all shifted about selfconsciously.

'Just softening you up, miss,' grinned Joey West.

'Yeah! That's it,' they all agreed.

'Mmmm, that's all very well,' she replied with mock seriousness, 'but no resting on your laurels or slipping back into wicked ways. You have to keep up all this good work.'

'Yes, Miss Drynan,' they repeated en masse, and began to file out of the classroom.

After one more admiring look Brooke carefully rewrapped the glass and returned it to its box, putting the box safely in her bag. She turned to follow the boys outside, only to find Drew leaning nonchalantly in the doorway.

'Did you really like our gift, Brooke?' he asked, his young face alight with pleasure.

'I loved it, Drew,' she replied honestly.

His face broke into a broad grin. 'I thought you would. I picked it out myself. The show went off well, too, didn't it?'

'It sure did, and it was a credit to you all,' she smiled. 'I'm very proud of the lot of you and your gift will always be a special and very happy memento of my stay here in the Towers.'

'Your stay here?' he repeated, his face sobering. 'You're not leaving, are you?'

'Not at the moment, but I could always be transferred next year or the year after that.'

'Oh. I never thought about you leaving,' he frowned. 'What if we don't want you to go?'

'I thought you didn't care much for teachers?' she laughed. 'If anyone overhears you, your reputation will be ruined, Drew Bastien. Anyway, don't worry about it now. Phew, it's hot!' She wiped her brow. 'I think I'll go across and have a cool drink. Want to join me?' she asked him.

'Sure. Good idea,' he smiled happily. 'If this do is running true to form, there'll be lemonade or lemon-ade.' He fell into step beside her as they crossed to the drink stand. 'Guaranteed not to make even the most ardent teetotaller more than slightly tipsy.'

They laughed together.

'You know, I think we even surprised ourselves with the show,' laughed Drew as they sipped the refreshing ice cold lemonade, 'but that's just between you and me,' he added with a conspiratorial wink.

'Is this a private party or can anyone join in?' asked a deep voice at Brooke's shoulder, causing her senses to leap alarmingly.

Drew turned slightly and his face lit up with surprised pleasure. 'Hey, Kley! I thought you wouldn't be able to make it. You should have been here earlier and seen our show. It was fantastic, wasn't it, Brooke?' He turned from his uncle to Brooke.

She nodded, wishing she could treat Kley MacLean with casual indifference.

'I did arrive in time to see the show,' Kley smiled at Drew, 'although I could only find standing room out here on the quadrangle. It sounded pretty good. If you hadn't told me all about it and I hadn't seen you all filing out I would never have believed it.'

'What do you mean, pretty good?' teased Drew. 'It was great.'

'I suppose you mean Brooke's choir of previously fallen angels,' remarked Dave, joining them. 'I call it a bloody miracle, if you'll pardon my colourful language.' He grabbed Drew's can of drink and took a gulp before Drew rescued it. 'Didn't know you'd be here, Kley. I thought you were up to your ears in cattle dipping.'

'I am—or I was—and I can assure you it never once went higher than my knees,' Kley pulled a face at Dave. 'I've left Dougal in charge as I particularly wanted to see how Drew's show came off, knowing the work and efforts he's put into it.' He glanced at Brooke and she found herself smiling involuntarily at him, thinking how nice he was in this relaxed mood.

'The boys have been just marvellous,' Brooke put her hand on Drew's shoulder. 'I knew they'd be a roaring success.'

'Such faith has the girl,' laughed Dave, 'and rightly so. Most of our fellow teachers are walking around in a state of disbelieving shock. They're more than sure that Brooke has 2AB under some hypnotic trance.'

Brooke laughed gaily. 'No criticism of my boys, if you please,' she championed her class. 'They're not so bad really. They only need the right kind of encouragement.'

Kley laughed, the sound vibrating through Brooke's

entire body, making her painfully aware of him and the effect he had on her. She might find his overbearing personality irritating, but she knew her senses responded to the virile masculinity of every sight and sound of him.

'I must say you're a generous soul.' Her eyes were fixed on the top button of his shirt, afraid to meet his gaze in case he read the responsive message that she knew was written in the depths of hers. But she could tell by his voice that he was still smiling. 'You can say that after having a cane toad planted in your chalk box?'

'Yuck!' Brooke shuddered.

'Did you tell Kley about that, Drew?' Dave turned to the boy, who blushed with embarrassment.

'Yes,' he looked sheepishly at Brooke. 'We had the room kind of booby trapped for our new teacher, you see, and when our new male teacher turned out to be Brooke—well, I didn't want to ... oh, heck, I couldn't let any of it happen to Brooke, so I removed our little welcomes. I didn't know about the toad or the duster, Brooke, honest. Otherwise I'd have got rid of them, too.'

Brooke laughed. 'Thank you anyway, Drew.'

'Tell me,' asked Kley, 'do you make a habit of picking up cane toads, Brooke? Most females of my acquaintance,' his tone was a little too condescending and Brooke's eyes sparked into his, 'would scream blue murder if faced with one of those grotesque little horrors.'

'Not Brooke,' said Dave, putting a hand around her waist. 'You're made of sterner stuff, aren't you, love?'

Kley's eyes narrowed and it seemed to Brooke that the temperature dropped by several degrees.

'Thanks for the vote of confidence, Dave, but I hope it was my first and last time. Ugh!' she said with feeling. 'It makes me shudder even now. And I think I've developed a phobia about chalk boxes. Now I'll wear a piece of chalk down to the elbow before I'll dig another piece out of the box.'

'If it's any consolation, Brooke,' laughed Drew, 'the fellows were full of admiration for you over that toad episode. They decided you weren't half bad.'

'See what one pretty face can achieve?' remarked Dave. His eyes ran over her figure in her cool cotton sundress, 'And—well, that'll do for starters,' he grinned.

'I'll drink to that,' remarked Kley, stepping across to the soft drink stand as the colour rose in Brooke's cheeks.

'Will Jacqui be coming with you to the dance this evening?' She turned quickly towards Dave, surprising a highly speculative look he was giving Kley.

'No, unfortunately she can't make it,' Dave frowned. 'Some design awards night she has to attend in Townsville, so I'll be alone.' He grinned to cover his disappointment. 'I think I'll make a complete nuisance of myself flirting outrageously with all the ladies, starting with you, Brooke.'

'You're a complete fraud, Dave Martin,' Brooke laughed softly.

'Ah, you see through me every time,' he looked rueful.

'It's a pity Jilly had to go to Hughenden this weekend for her friend's twenty-first birthday party, isn't it? The dance after the fête is always a huge success, according to the others, and Jilly's always the life of the party,' she remarked, one part of her waiting for Kley's return.

'She sure is.' Dave looked up as Kley rejoined them. 'You're coming to the dance, aren't you, Kley?'

Brooke found herself holding her breath waiting for his reply.

'Yes, I think I will. Drew pressured me into buying a ticket, so I may as well take advantage of it.' Kley turned to Brooke. 'May I offer you a lift to the hall this evening to save you taking your car?'

It was hard to say who looked the more surprised by his offer, Brooke or Dave, and it was several seconds before Brooke could find her voice to answer him. 'Well, thank you very much, but I'm going along early with the Masons. There'll be some last-minute arrangements to see to and John Mason asked me to help Ann out with them. I'm free once the dance begins, so I'll see you there,' she finished lamely.

'I bet you're going to be the most popular girl there, Brooke,' Drew remarked, reminding them that he was still standing there, 'so save a dance for me, won't you?'

His uncle raised one eyebrow in his nephew's direction.

'Listen to the cheek of him!' exclaimed Dave. 'You'll have to stand in line behind me. Age before beauty, mate,' he grinned.

A couple of her fellow teachers joined them to congratulate Brooke on 2AB's success and soon she was drawn away to look at some of the other class exhibits. Although she caught a couple of quick glimpses of Kley in the crowd attending the fête she didn't see him to speak to before she left for home to get ready for the dance.

CHAPTER TEN

THE music stopped and Kley's hands fell to his side. It had been over an hour since his arrival at the hall before he had approached Brooke to ask her to dance with him, and although her nerve ends had stretched to fever pitch while she waited for him to come, she had been so keyed up that now she was all but wishing that the dance was over. The fact that he hadn't spoken one word to her as they moved conventionally around the floor hadn't helped her nervous system to regain its equilibrium.

'Hey, Kley! Kley!' called Drew, pulling a young girl along with him as he weaved in and out of the couples waiting for the music to recommence. 'What's with that old-fashioned dancing?' He stood stiffly with his arms extended, causing a wave of laughter from those nearby. 'Don't you dig the disco beat, Broo . . . Miss Drynan?' he grinned at Brooke.

Away from the disorientating quality of Kley's disturbing touch Brooke relaxed a little and smiled back at Drew's challenge. 'I'll have you know, Drew Bastien, that I have in my possession a cup which I won in my era's equivalent of a disco dancing competition. You're talking to an expert.'

'My, my, we are impressed, Miss Drynan, but talk's cheap. We want proof, don't we, gang?' he appealed to his cronies, and received an affirmative chorus.

Brooke glanced at Kley, an impish smile dimpling her cheeks. 'Are you game, Mr MacLean?' she teased.

Kley inclined his head. 'Never let it be said that I allowed a lady's challenge to pass unrecognised,' he said amicably enough, although his eyes seemed to hold a hint of warning.

The beat began and, feeling lightheaded, Brooke moved slowly until she began to feel the rhythm. Then she threw herself into the energetic gyrations of the dance. Kley followed her lead with admirable ability, cheered on by Drew and his mates, until they all joined in, each giving a little of his own variation to the performance.

The bracket eventually came to a crescendous end and Kley wordlessly passed Brooke his snowy white handkerchief warm from its position close to his body in the breast pocket of his lightweight safari suit jacket. She dabbed the light film of perspiration from her forehead and when she returned the handkerchief he wiped his own brow.

'I don't know how they can keep up this pace all night,' he remarked, 'or how I let you goad me into a bout of it.' He loosened the knot of his tie as the band struck up a slow ballad.

Not waiting for her comment, he drew her into a more conventional hold. 'This is more like it,' he said softly, drawing her closer until his breath fanned her hair and she could feel the hardness of his thighs against her body.

Momentarily she held herself tense and restrained in his arms, but the nearness of his body and the slow sensuousness of the dance seemed to thaw her reserve and soon she had relaxed against him. All their previous antagonisms had faded, or at least were shelved for the night, and pushing the niggling memories to the back of her mind, she allowed her traitorous body to convince her that this one night of lowered defences did not mean she had conceded the battle.

Tonight she was wearing her favourite dress, the rich green jersey material hugging her figure to perfection. The neckline formed a deep V, hinting at the rising fullness of her breasts, while the back plunged moderately to display her nicely tanned skin to perfection. The colour of the dress enhanced the golden highlights in her hair and the knowledge that she knew she looked more than passably attractive lent a glow of excitement to her cheeks.

When the slow bracket drew to a close she moved reluctantly apart from Kley, feeling suddenly loath to break the sympathetic and highly responsive bond that had grown between them. That he was fully aware of it she read in the intenseness of his deep blue eyes.

'My turn, Kley, old buddy.' Dave's voice broke the web that had woven itself about the couple on the dance floor. 'You've been monopolising the dishiest-looking bird in the hall for long enough. The rest of us are planning a revolution and I'm the first assault. May I have the pleasure, Miss Drynan?' He bowed in Brooke's direction.

She cast a quick glance at Kley before answering.

He smiled a little stiffly. 'I suppose I must concede defeat this time. Thanks for the dance, Brooke. I'll see you later.' He put a friendly hand on Dave's shoulder and was gone.

The remainder of the evening flew by, having taken on a sensation of unreality for Brooke. She danced with Dave a couple of times, with Drew hilariously once, and with various colleagues from school.

Of Kley she saw very little. A couple of times she caught sight of him watching the dancers and once or twice they passed on the dance floor, but in the last hour or so he seemed to have disappeared completely. Perhaps he had left already. Her spirits sank at the thought of not seeing him again before the evening drew to a close.

Now it was nearing midnight and she stood talking to Dave and Drew, all the while keeping an eye peeled for any sign that the Masons were ready to leave. She wanted to ask Dave if Kley was still here, but somehow she couldn't face one of Dave's knowing smiles.

'There's Kley now,' pointed Drew, and they all turned to see him approach Ann Mason, speak to her for a few moments, and then, inevitably, he was striding purposefully across to join them.

'Ready to go?' Dave asked, stifling a yawn.

Kley nodded. 'You take Drew home, will you, Dave, and I'll drop Brooke off.' He turned to Brooke. 'I've told Ann she needn't worry about waiting for you. They're leaving the cleaning up of the hall until tomorrow.'

Brooke's eyes returned to Ann Mason. She and her husband were about to leave the hall and Ann raised her hand to wave goodbye. Apparently everyone seemed to take it for granted that she would want to go home with Kley, when in reality she. . . . Brooke swallowed quickly. She didn't want to go home with him. Did she?

Dave glanced thoughtfully from Brooke to Kley. 'Are you driving back out to the Downs now?' was all he asked, although Brooke had a feeling that wasn't really what was on his mind.

'No, I think not.' Kley rubbed a hand wearily around the back of his neck. 'After all this strenuous activity I don't feel much like dodging roos tonight. I'll stay at Peg's and drive home in the morning, so leave the door unlatched for me, will you?'

'Okay, then. Well, I'll see you, Brooke.' Dave turned to the boy. 'Come on, Drew.'

'My car's over here,' said Kley as Dave and Drew left them at the door of the hall.

Brooke nodded and followed him along the footpath to where he had left his Ford utility. She had to practically run to keep up with his long strides and by the time she had reached the car she was quite breathless and felt a stirring of anger.

He unlocked the door and held it open for her, and, in the glow of the overhead street lighting, his face was all planes and angles in an expression of cool detachment.

Sliding into the passenger side, she noticed aloofly

that a clean cotton seat cover had been placed on the seat, almost as though he knew he would be taking someone home this evening. She wondered if he had had anyone in particular in mind or whether any female would have done. Her anger grew as she watched him remove his safari suit jacket and stow it on the back parcel shelf before settling beside her and guiding the car in a quick precision U-turn in a break in the traffic.

He drove quickly and neither of them spoke in the short time it took to reach her flat, and Brooke decided angrily that he obviously hadn't wanted it to be her that he was escorting home. Well, she hadn't wanted him to take her home and she hadn't asked him to. She should have gone home with the Masons as she had planned.

Kley pulled the utility smoothly into the kerb in front of her flat and, slipping the gears into neutral, left the engine idling, further fanning the flame of Brooke's ire.

'Thank you for driving me home,' she said coolly. 'I'd ask you in for coffee, but I know you're in a hurry to get home,' she finished, barely disguising her sarcasm.

He reached out and switched off the ignition, removing the keys. 'There's no hurry. Make it a cup of tea and it's a deal.' He climbed out of the utility and walked around to open her door.

She led the way along the path and up the steps to the door of her flat and, in the darkness, she chastised herself severely. Now she had to spend more time with him, and this time alone. Well, it jolly well served her right for issuing rash invitations.

Her keys had managed to work their way into the corner of her purse and when she eventually found them she fumbled around in the dimness trying to find the lock. A firm hand reached out and covered her own, removing the keys from her nerveless fingers and finding the lock with one decisive movement. Then the door swung open and Kley had flicked on the light, standing back for her to precede him inside.

Brooke hurried across to the kitchen and filled the

electric kettle. When she turned around with two cups and saucers for the tea Kley had seated himself on a stool on the other side of the breakfast bar. Forcing herself to relax, Brooke lifted the milk jug from the refrigerator and set it beside the cups.

'It's not a bad sized flat, is it?' he remarked casually, looking around.

'Yes. It's quite roomy. Having the living room and kitchen open like this gives the impression that it's even larger than it actually is.' She poured boiling water on to the tea leaves and set the pot on the breakfast bar. 'It will seem even bigger when Jilly moves back to Townsville next weekend. How do you like your tea?' she asked, perching nervously on a matching stool on the opposite side of the bench.

'Strong and white with two sugars, please,' he replied evenly, and she poured the tea in silence.

'You'll find the place will seem deadly quiet when Jilly goes,' he said, absently stirring his tea.

'Yes. No one could possibly feel lonely with Jilly around. I lived with my family down south, so Jilly's presence helped bridge the gap there. I guess I mostly miss the family discussions at mealtimes—and the squabbles,' she added, feeling on relatively safe ground. 'However, teaching keeps me busy, so I don't get a lot of spare time to miss them too much.'

And then she found herself talking easily about her family. How Mike was a qualified motor mechanic and was restoring an ancient Jaguar, and about Renee's occupation as a dental assistant. 'Craig, the youngest, is a little older than Drew and I'm afraid he finds his lack of years a colossal cross to bear,' she laughed.

Kley declined her offer of another cup of tea, so she picked up their cups and rinsed them under the tap, leaving them to dry on the draining board. When she turned back to Kley he was standing in front of her bookcase, his hands in his pockets, looking at the titles of her books. He had left his jacket in the car and the material of his pale blue shirt stretched across the muscles of his shoulders and back, hugging the taper of his body down into the narrow waist of his trousers.

'This is your family?' he indicated a framed photograph on the top of the bookcase.

Moving into the living room and keeping as much distance as possible between them, she pointed out each member of her family. However, she was becoming increasingly aware of the force of his magnetism, and turned nervously to show him the glass that Drew had presented to her that afternoon, half wishing that they could return to their open conflict rather than this heady explosive watchfulness.

'See what 2AB gave me for helping them with their concert. It's beautiful, isn't it? Actually, Drew told me he chose it himself.'

Kley lifted the glass, turned it over in his hands and set it back on the shelf. 'You're working wonders with my nephew. He's changed considerably these past weeks, the difference in him is quite noticeable.' He picked up another small ornament and absently replaced it. 'All in all he's been a handful, and I guess I haven't had the time to spend with him that I should have.' He paused. 'You've made quite a hit with Drew,' he added, not looking at her.

Brooke smiled. 'I like Drew. He's a nice boy.'

'Dougal likes you, too,' he said. 'I guess it must be almost an epidemic in the area.'

All of a sudden the tension between them intensified.

'What ... what must?' she asked quietly, her voice strangely not her own.

'You,' he replied, 'being a hit with every male for miles around, be he six or sixty.'

Somehow she wasn't surprised when his fingers took hold of her wrist, sending shivers of fire through her as he turned her towards him. Her mouth was dry as she remained motionless, her eyes fixed on the knot of his tie where he had loosened it and undone the top button of his shirt, showing the start of his strong chest covered in fine dark hair.

His hand moved up her arm and then his fingers were lifting a silken curl, watching its burnished shine in the artificial light as he moved it back and forth on his finger. When his hand moved to the nape of her neck it required only the slightest pressure from him to bring her closer to his sinewy hardness.

For Brooke time had stood still, was motionless. If she breathed she accomplished it unconsciously. Kley lifted his other hand to cup her cheek, his eyes moving slowly and deliberately over her face, taking in each feature, as though committing it indelibly upon his memory. Her brow, her eyes, her nose, settling disturbingly on her lips until they burned for the touch of his. Her lips quivered as he traced their outline with the feather-soft touch of his thumb.

And then he bent to touch her lips with his, gently, tentatively, until her eyes closed and she melted against him. She gave a soft half sigh, half moan, and he pulled her closer to him, moulding her body to every line and angle of his, his lips taking possession of hers, forcing them apart, probing, drawing a response from the depths of her being.

No other man had ever kissed her in such a manner—or perhaps it was that no one before Kley had ever stormed the wall of her defences and drawn forth such a tide of response from her very soul.

His lips reluctantly released hers and moved across her cheek over her eyelids, teased her earlobe until she took his face in her hands, so that his lips could claim hers again.

'God, Brooke, you don't know how often I've wanted to hold you like this, touch you, kiss you like this since that morning on the riverbank.' His fingers moved in her hair. 'I haven't slept nights for thinking about it, and when I do sleep you haunt my dreams,' he murmured hoarsely.

His passionate words had the blaze of her desire spreading the length of her body. Sliding her hands around his neck, she moved her fingers sensuously through the dark thickness of his hair, making him murmur her name against her lips, drawing her still closer against his hardening muscles.

Lifting her effortlessly up into his arms, he moved to the couch and sat down, pulling her on to his knee. He put his lips to her arm, moving slowly up to her shoulder, across the materials of her dress to her throat, lingering in the sweetness, continuing slowly around to the hollow at the front where a pulse beat in rhythm with her heart, and downwards to the beginning of the vale between her breasts, only to be halted by the buttoned neckline.

Strong brown fingers were drawn to the buttons and then his lips continued their progress, lower, sending her blood pounding through her veins. His lips moved again, blazing a trail of fire up to her earlobe, across her shoulder, pushing aside her dress and exposing a firm round breast.

As Kley caressed her Brooke could feel her resistance ebbing away and she could sense that the tight control he had on himself was also in danger of crumbling under the force of their rising passion.

Gently she pushed him away. 'Kley,' she murmured.

'Mmm,' he replied huskily, letting his lips rove over her chin to play with her mouth that throbbed anew at his touch.

'Kley,' she began again, fighting the emotional urge to let herself be carried away on the tide of his love-making. 'Kley, we shouldn't. . . .'

'Shouldn't what?' he asked sensuously, caressing her so that she could scarcely think coherently.

'Kley . . . I know you're very experienced,' began the last stand in her defences as her body cried for complete surrender to his demands. 'That is, everyone says that you're. . . .'

He slowly raised his head. His eyes had changed colour, were slightly colder, although his lips still retained their sensual curve. 'Do you want to know whether I caress every girl like this? Is that it?' he asked harshly.

'No,' Brooke cried indignantly, while the mental picture she conjured up of Kley in the arms of other faceless women tore through her heart like a sword-thrust. 'It's only that—well, everyone seems to be of the opinion that. . . .'

'You should know by now how nosey everyone,' he emphasised, 'is in an isolated area like this. And you shouldn't believe all you hear. When there aren't any stories forthcoming people have a tendency to manufacture them, create their own facts. It helps to break the monotony.'

His eyes burned into hers. 'If I carried on with half the females everyone ties me up with then I'd be hard pressed to find time to even visit the Downs. Let's just leave it that I haven't lived the life of a monk and, in return, I won't ask you for a detailed account of the list of your conquests,' he finished cruelly, taking savage, almost primitive possession of her lips, forcing her back against the couch, pinning her body with the weight of his.

She struggled against him, but she was no match for his superior male strength. In fact, her struggles only served to inflame him all the more. With a sob she stopped fighting, and when her passivity reached him he raised his head to look at her tear-streaked face.

'There haven't been any,' she said through lips swollen from his kisses, her voice but a whisper.

Kley frowned. 'Haven't been any what?'

'Men in my life before . . . before you,' she replied, her gaze on his chin. 'I mean, I guess Dave told you I was engaged once, but we didn't . . . I've never. . . .' Her voice faded away and she was unaware of the vulnerability in the soft transparency of the eyes she raised to his, half afraid of what she would read there.

He looked at her for seconds, or maybe minutes, before he sighed and gently rearranged her bodice, his hand lingering momentarily on the aching fullness of her breast. Then he was standing, apart from her, and she was free. But it was a hollow freedom, more like a severance. Turning away from her, he began tucking his shirt back into the waistband of his trousers.

'Kley, I'm sorry,' she said softly, getting to her feet, knowing that what she had said had needed to be said. She went to him, wrapping her arms about his waist, holding him convulsively. Her arms slid up around his neck, drawing his lips easily back to join hers, wanting him to hold her as he had before, yearning to give him pleasure, needing the satisfaction only complete surrender would give.

His lips responded to hers fleetingly and then he put her firmly from him. And when she would have moved back into his arms he held her away, although she knew instinctively the effort it took him to do just that.

'No, Brooke—please. Stay there.' His voice sounded a little hoarse. 'We both know,' his breathing was ragged, as though he had been running, 'how close we came to taking a step we'd both regret, for differing reasons, tomorrow and,' he stopped, taking another steadying breath, 'I still wouldn't trust me if I were you.'

'Kley, I'm sorry.' A whisper was all she could manage, tears slipping down her cheeks.

He turned from her as though those tears could be his undoing and ran his fingers unsteadily through his hair. 'Look, all this, it's not your fault,' he said quietly, expressionlessly. He paused and walked over to her bookcase again, staring at the glass the boys had given her. 'I knew it would be inevitable if I came in with you tonight.'

Suddenly he turned to face her, his hands in his pockets, straining the light material across the firmness of his thighs. 'I'll admit my intentions tonight were far from honourable. And nor were they unpremeditated.'

He laughed bitterly. 'I thought I could handle it. I was going to have the last laugh, Brooke.' His expression was all self-derision and he began to pace up and down the suddenly small living room, then he stopped in front of her, although keeping his distance.

'I also admit, without wishing to sound immodest, that in the past I could usually have any woman I wanted.' His eyes pierced hers. 'And believe me, Brooke, I wanted you. From the moment I saw you with Dave's hands holding you up on that chair, I wanted you.' He dragged his eyes away. 'And I burned with jealous rage every time Dave went near you. I wasn't used to sharing. But you made it very plain you weren't interested.' He sighed. 'It was a new and somewhat irritating feeling for me, but I had every confidence that I could change your mind. Then I overheard you making your wager with Jilly.'

He turned to look at her again and Brooke blushed with shame. 'No woman has ever. . . .' His nostrils flared in remembered anger and then he grimaced. 'Well, it stuck in my mind like a piece of spear grass gets under your skin, and like that sliver of spear grass, it began to fester there.'

'Kley. . . .' Brooke began earnestly, but he held up his hand.

'No, let me finish. I decided I'd lead you on, let you think you'd won the bet and then, at the last minute— tonight,' he said wryly, 'I was going to turn the tables on you.' He looked at her intensely, his eyes moving over her ravenously, as though he couldn't stop himself. 'I couldn't even tell you when pretence ended and reality began, but I somehow think it's all rebounded on me.'

He walked across and stood looking down at her, his expression making her knees tremble.

Well, you've won, said a small voice inside her. The great Kley MacLean had been brought down. He even admitted it himself.

So why wasn't she rejoicing? Hadn't she wanted to

see him taken down a peg, watch his ego crack? Then why was she experiencing his pain deep within her, in the region of her heart? Wasn't this what she'd wanted? Somehow the sweetness of victory had turned disastrously sour.

'Kley, that bet, it was just a spur of the moment joke,' she began, and another tear slipped from her lashes and rolled down her cheek.

His finger caught the droplet, his expression softening. Brooke thought he was about to take her in his arms again, but he turned away with a sigh, stopping when he had opened the door of her flat.

'Tell Jilly she owes you a dollar,' he said softly, and was gone.

CHAPTER ELEVEN

AWAKENING next morning with a blinding headache Brooke groaned at the thought of a trip down to the hall to face a cleaning up session, but she had promised Ann Mason she would go along to give her a hand.

After Kley had left she had tossed restlessly for hours, reliving the moments of ecstasy and despair. In the darkness of the night it seemed that her happiness was slipping through her fingers before she had barely tasted its sweetness.

If only she could relive those few moments with Jilly and wipe out those idle words! Kley must have a very low opinion of her if he thought she went around making outrageous bets. Tears had fallen again.

She hadn't known a moment's peace, she exaggerated, since she had met Kley MacLean, anger momentarily replacing despair. Why had she allowed herself to leave her secure world in Brisbane? Perhaps she had only been half alive, at least she hadn't had to suffer the pain of knowing Kley's feelings for her stemmed from a desire for revenge.

And what about your feelings for him? she asked herself. And all at once she was loath to analyse them. But they had begun with a need to teach Kley a lesson, so wasn't that as bad as his motives for revenge? In the beginning it had all seemed such a joke, and she wouldn't have worried about his feelings at all. But now. . . . Now his pain was her pain, and cold fingers of foreboding encircled her heart, filling her with an aching hollowness of loss.

She dozed fitfully at last until her alarm roused her to reluctant wakefulness. Dragging herself out of bed, she splashed her eyes with tepid water, trying to erase the ravages resulting from her tears.

Although Anne gave her a puzzled look she made no comment but chatted happily about the success of the dance, her undemanding company doing much to soothe Brooke's troubled mind.

The days turned into a week and, as each day passed, so too fell Brooke's spirits. In the beginning she had expected Kley to phone, allowing herself the faint hope that he would contact her. But she heard no word. Even Dave's teasing banter was conspicuous by its absence when their paths crossed at school.

She had made no mention of any part of the aftermath of the dance to Jilly, but she knew the other girl watched her curiously. However, when Brooke fobbed off any tentative enquiries that she made Jilly asked no more questions, respecting Brooke's reluctance to discuss her problem. Jilly was a true friend, having the knack of knowing when to tease and when not to probe too deeply.

The weekend came and went with no word from him, and so the spark of hope within Brooke withered and died. Drew seemed to be the only one able to mention Kley's name with any casualness, and it was from him that she heard that his uncle had been out on the property for days looking into a suspected outbreak of some form of cattle disease and no one seemed to know when he would be back. Jilly's departure for Townsville to relieve at Pimlico High School had left an empty void in the flat that Brooke found almost unbearable.

Wednesday evening found her sitting dejectedly pushing the meal she had prepared for herself around her plate. A large tear rolled down to her chin and on to her hand and she closed her eyes, about to give way to a bout of self-pity. Irritably she brushed away the tears with the back of her hand, valiantly pulling herself together.

This would have to stop. Soon her depression would begin affecting her work. In fact, today she had felt the restlessness of the boys when she knew she was only giving her lesson part of her attention.

Clearing away the dishes, she decided to give the whole flat a clean-up, scrub and polish the floors, re-arrange the furniture, put everything from her mind except the job on hand. She changed into a pair of old faded jeans and T-shirt, tied her hair up into two slightly askew pigtails and was on her way to collect her cleaning utensils when the doorbell rang.

Kley. Her heart began to race and it was a few seconds before she could move towards the door. Taking a steadying breath, she opened the door and Dave stepped inside, one hand holding a frosty bottle of champagne and the other arm wrapping itself around Brooke's waist, twirling her around until she was giddy.

'Dave, for heaven's sake!' she gasped. 'What's all this in aid of?'

'In aid of?' He set her free. 'When I tell you my news you'll understand. Got a couple of bubbly glasses? You're going to help me celebrate!'

Brooke opened a cupboard and took out two of her best glasses, setting them on the bench top. Dave removed the top from the bottle of champagne and she ducked as it popped, sending the top catapulting over her head. Dave laughingly filled the glasses, passing one to Brooke and holding one himself.

'To Jacqui and me.' He raised his glass. 'May our second attempt at marriage outlast the first,' he grinned, and they took a sip of champagne.

'Dave, that's great news!' Brooke rubbed her nose as the bubbles rose from her glass. 'When did all this come about?'

'Jacqui phoned me earlier on.' He sat down on the bar stool. 'We'd pretty well decided to give it another go by last weekend, but there was still the matter of Jacqui's shop in Townsville. I didn't want to make any stipulation that she should give it up or sell it.' He took another sip of champagne. 'Anyway, she told me tonight she's decided to let her senior assistant manage it for her as she's coming to the Towers to be with me. She'll only need to go back to Townsville a couple of times a month and she'll still retain an interest in the shop. Brooke, can you imagine how happy I am?' he asked earnestly, and impulsively he leant across the breakfast bar to give her a hug, upsetting his champagne glass in the process, the liquid soaking the front of his shirt.

'Blast!' He pulled the wet material out from his skin. 'Sorry I was so clumsy, Brooke.'

She reached for the dishcloth, laughing at his rueful expression. 'Never mind. No harm done and there's more in the bottle. You'd better go into the bathroom and squeeze most of it out of your shirt. There's a dry towel behind the door, use that.'

Dave disappeared through the bedroom door muttering to himself while she wiped down the bench top, refilling his overturned glass and setting the bottle in the fridge to keep it cool.

She was walking towards the bedroom to see if Dave needed any help when the doorbell pealed for the second time.

'Hello, Brooke. I'm sorry to call so late, I've been to a meeting concerning the organisation of the rodeo next weekend and, as usual, the meeting ran longer than I'd anticipated.' Kley's eyes, faintly guarded, took in her faded jeans, clinging T-shirt and, by now, flushed face. 'May I come in?'

Completely forgetting Dave's presence, she stepped back for him to enter. He looked so vitally attractive in his dark blue slacks and cream open-necked knit shirt that she was robbed of speech, her breath knotting in her throat.

'We had the stock arrangements to finalise,' he told her. 'The Downs usually supplies most of the broncos.'

'Yes, Drew was telling me about it yesterday,' she said, wishing she could be in his arms instead of standing tensely, mouthing civilities.

He nodded. 'I suppose he also told you he wants to compete in the junior buck jumping event. I was competing myself at his age, but I feel a little hesitant about letting him enter.' His deep incredibly blue eyes looked into hers, and she wondered how she had ever thought she disliked him. 'I was wondering whether you'd thought of going to the rodeo. Perhaps you'd like to come . . .?'

His last words remained unsaid as Dave emerged from the bedroom, tucking his opened shirt into his pants. 'There, reasonably respectable again. Kley!' He was no less surprised to see his friend than Kley was to see him.

'Hey! If I'd known you were in town . . .' Dave began, his smile fading as his friend's eyes raked him from head to foot.

Brooke watched in horror as a cold mask settled on Kley's face and a nerve in his cheek jumped as his jaw tightened, his hands balled into fists.

Dave looked from Kley to Brooke's pale face. 'Hey, Kley! Now wait a minute. . . .'

'I must be off,' Kley bit out icily. 'I promised Drew I'd call to see him before I returned to the Downs.' He strode towards the door while Brooke could only stand aghast. 'I'll see you, Dave. Brooke.' He nodded grimly at her, his eyes flicking over her so brutally that she flinched. And he was gone before she could collect herself.

Brooke looked at Dave and subsided into the nearest beanbag and wept.

'Hell, Brooke, don't cry.' Dave pulled her awkwardly to her feet and into his arms, patting her gently on the shoulder until her sobs had subsided.

With a sigh she pushed herself away from the dampness of his chest. 'I'm sorry, Dave. I'm spoiling your celebration.' She moved back to the breakfast bar and handed him his drink, taking such a gulp of her own that she had to cough to catch her breath.

Dave smiled crookedly at her when she met his eyes.

'We're a couple of blind fools, aren't we?' he said, setting his glass back on the bench. 'And I guess I'll have to go after another fool and explain the situation to him before he lays me out with one king hit.' He patted her hand. 'Don't worry, Brooke. I'll sort it out with Kley.' He paused at the door. 'He doesn't usually jump to lurid conclusions. I think the big green monster has got him where it hurts.' He winked at her. 'And he's one hell of a lucky guy!'

On Saturday morning Brooke was undecided as to whether she should do her usual weekly shopping or remain at the flat. She had not heard from Kley, although Dave had said he had sorted the whole episode out with his friend. After pottering dejectedly about the flat she fetched her purse and car keys and, in exasperation, drove down to the shopping centre.

It wasn't as busy as it normally was and she concluded that a lot of people had obviously gone to the rodeo. She purchased her groceries, spoke to one or two parents who were also shopping and wandered slowly back towards her car, glancing in the shop windows, some already festooned with Christmas decorations. She supposed she should be thinking about going home for the holidays. Her parents would be disappointed if she didn't.

She almost collided with a tall red-haired man, father of the Andrews twins, before she even noticed him.

'I'm sorry, Mr Andrews,' she apologised as he righted her parcel of groceries which she had almost upended on to the footpath. 'How are you?'

'Fine, Miss Drynan, just fine. I'm off to collect my wife and the boys and we're going to the rodeo. Are you going along yourself?' he asked.

'I . . . I may go this afternoon,' she replied.

'Good. You'll enjoy it, We all put in an appearance every year. Quite an event for the Towersites is the rodeo. And the young lads look forward to entering the rough riding events. The twins have been pressuring me for the last few years to let them have a go. I always tell them they'll break their young necks, that's for sure,' he laughed.

'Do they have many accidents?' Brooke asked, her mind going immediately to Kley.

'No, only bumps and bruises and dented prides. Although I did hear a fellow say that someone from Terebori Downs had been taken to hospital about an hour ago.'

Brooke felt the blood leave her face. She was so pale that Mr Andrews took her arm in consternation.

'Are you feeling ill, Miss Drynan?' he asked worriedly.

'No, no, I'll be all right. I . . . did you say someone from Terebori Downs had been injured?' Brooke asked breathlessly.

'Yes, I'm sure it was Terebori Downs,' Mr Andrews watched her pale face turn even whiter. 'I think you'd better sit down, Miss Drynan,' he said, looking helplessly for somewhere for her to do just that.

Brooke stood rigidly. 'No, I'm fine now. My . . . my car's just here. I'll be off now. It was nice seeing you.' She fumbled distractedly for her keys.

Mr Andrews watched until she had pulled away from the kerb before shaking his head and continuing on his way.

In the short time it took her to drive up to the hospital Brooke's imagination had conjured up all sorts of possibilities with regard to Kley's injuries, none of them in any way soothing to her nervous system.

Having parked the car, she was looking around agitatedly for a sign directing her to Casualty when Joey West appeared around the corner of the nearest building, a piece of plaster stuck across his cheek.

'Joey!' she almost fell on him with relief. 'Where do I find Casualty?'

'Next building over,' he said. 'I've just come from there. I took a tumble off a bronco,' he added proudly, indicating his wound.

'Are you all right?' she asked.

'Sure,' he said offhandedly. 'It's just a scratch, but Mum panicked. You should see. . . .'

'Joey, you haven't heard how Kley . . . Mr MacLean is, have you?' she asked quickly.

'Mr MacLean? Fine, as far as I know. Why?' he frowned.

'He was injured at the rodeo, too,' she told him as the boy's father's car pulled into the kerb to collect him.

'Miss Drynan, I think there must be some mistake,' Joey began, but Brooke was striding off in the direction he had pointed out, calling a hasty goodbye.

Hurrying up to the reception desk, she waited impatiently for the nurse on duty to finish assisting a woman with a fractious baby.

The nurse eventually turned to Brooke. 'Can I help you?'

'Could I see Mr MacLean, please? I believe he came in some time ago?' Brooke's stomach tensed in nervous dread.

'Oh, yes. Mr MacLean from Terebori Downs and the young lad.' The nurse consulted her book frowningly, causing Brooke's heart to skip a beat. 'They've gone up to Lissner Ward, room number three. Follow that path outside to your right and it's the second building, bottom floor.'

Brooke thanked her and found the ward in no time. The Sister on duty was away from her desk, so Brooke barged along the corridor searching for the room number. She was almost to the end of the hall when a door up ahead opened and Kley walked out. A very whole and healthy Kley, who stopped short in surprise when he saw her.

His appearance, minus any disfigurement or bandages, had pulled Brooke to a halt as well and she leaned weakly against the wall in shock and relief.

'Are you all right, Brooke?' He was beside her, taking her arm.

She nodded helplessly, feeling tears rush to her eyes. 'I . . . I thought you'd been hurt at the rodeo. Someone said you'd been rushed to the hospital.'

'There you go again, listening to idle rumours,' he said softly, almost caressingly. 'Not me—Drew.' Kley's arms moved around her and she leant thankfully against his firm chest, feeling the strong beat of his heart. 'The young devil let himself get tossed and trodden on by a bull. After I told him he could only enter the bronco event, too.'

'Drew? Is he badly hurt?'

'He's had his leg plastered and he's resting comfortably,' Kley grimaced, and then looked down into her eyes. 'You'd have been upset if it had been my unworthy hide?' His voice was light, but his eyes watched her closely.

Brooke closed her eyes, unable to answer.

He went to draw her closer into his arms and then realised they were in the hallway of the hospital ward and, taking her arm, led her outside to the car park.

'Where are we going?' she pulled herself together long enough to ask as he put her into his utility.

'You'll see,' was all he said.

'But what about Drew?'

'Drew's on top of the world,' he grinned. 'He's got two young nurses doting on him!'

Fifteen minutes later he switched off the ignition in the layby overlooking the Burdekin River.

Kley sighed, resting his arms on the steering wheel before turning slowly to look at Brooke. Her pulses began to race, fired by the look in his eyes coupled with the memories this place evoked, the flame fanned by her feelings for him, which at that precise moment threatened to overcome her. She couldn't meet his eyes and her gaze fell to her lap where her fingers pulled nervously at the buttons down the front of her skirt.

The creaking protest of the seat as he shifted his weight closer to her made her dart a look at him.

'Oh, Brooke,' he murmured huskily, and his lips met hers in a blinding kiss. When he drew away they were both breathless. Somehow he had lifted her on to his knees and her arms were around his neck, her fingers moving in his thick dark hair.

'God, Brooke, how I want you,' he said huskily. 'That night, after the dance, if you only knew how close I came to staying! I had a feeling I'd never be the same again.' His eyes moved expressively from her lips, soft and yielding from his kisses, down to the neckline of her short-sleeved knit top which moulded her full breasts still tingling from his caresses.

'I thought you were angry with me.' Brooke's lips trembled invitingly.

'Never with you,' he replied, tearing his eyes away from her invitation. 'My anger was directed at myself for allowing my emotions to get out of control. That was a novel and quite shattering experience for me and I very nearly couldn't handle it.' One hand cupped her cheek. 'Remember how I teased you about my Achilles' heel? Well, you found mine without even trying,' he put her hand against the beat of his heart, 'right here.'

Taking a shuddering breath, he looked deeply into her eyes. 'Believe me, I've worked like a Trojan these past two weeks trying to keep away from you, but it tore me apart.' He kissed her again, almost savagely, and she responded with all the fervour of her love for him, their embrace laying bare their longing for each other.

'The other night I really felt you never wanted to see me again,' she said shakily as they gazed at each other in wonderment.

He laughed softly, 'No way!' and hugged her to him. 'I'd be an empty shell without you.' His voice was low with sincerity and tears of happiness trembled on her lashes. 'I love you, Brooke. How soon will you marry me? I don't think I can last out much longer not being able to touch you, caress you, kiss you like this.' His mouth teased her earlobe, her jawline and lastly and lovingly, her lips.

'Kley.' She moved so that she could look at him. 'Are you sure you want to marry me? I mean, that business of the bet with Jilly and—well, if I hadn't come to the hospital. . . .'

He silenced her with a quick kiss. 'You, my love, are going to have a hard time explaining that bet to our grandchildren,' he teased. 'And as to the rodeo, I was about to come to collect you this morning when Drew had his fall,' he said quietly, shifting her more comfortably on his knee, 'and I was hoping you'd still want to come along with me.' The corners of his mouth lifted. 'No, that's not strictly true. I was going to tell you you were coming with me and that was that,' he said with some of his old arrogance.

And suddenly Brooke's heart was singing and a dimple appeared in her cheek. 'If you'd said that as late as a week ago you'd have had a battle on your hands, Kley MacLean!'

He chuckled. 'Don't I know it!' He traced the line of her nose to her lips with the tip of one finger. 'I used to watch for the flashes in those beautiful blue eyes of yours.'

'I'm glad you were going to ask me to the rodeo, but I was sure you'd changed your mind when you found Dave at the flat,' she said, her fingers smoothing the collar of his shirt, moving inside to touch the hair-roughened skin.

Kley sighed. 'On Wednesday night I was as jealous as hell.' His eyes burned into hers. 'I told myself I had no right to expect you to have no other men friends, especially after the way I'd treated you, but it didn't help. If I'd stayed I'd have. . . .' He took a deep breath. 'When Dave walked out of your bedroom I could have killed you both.' His eyes closed in pain. 'I was blind to anything but my own conclusions. I think that was the worst moment of my life. Dave's my best friend and if you wanted him, well . . . but I was so jealous I couldn't think straight.' His arms tightened about her.

'Dave . . . he did explain?' she asked, and he nodded.

'Called me all kinds of a jealous fool—and that,' he kissed the tip of her nose, 'is exactly what I was. When I left your flat I went to Peg's—I still don't remember how I got there—and I was in one hell of a temper. Dave arrived and manhandled me downstairs to cool me off and while I was doing that he put me in the picture. Told me you were absolutely head over heels in love with me,' he grinned at her outraged expression.

'Oh, he did, did he?'

'He most certainly did. That was the only thing that stopped me from flattening him.' He looked at her gently. 'He also told me about your fiancé marrying your cousin. This chap Marsh? He broke your engagement?'

Brooke nodded.

'The fellow must have been mad!' he ejaculated, causing Brooke to laugh delightedly.

Kley lifted her hand and touched his lips to her palm. 'But because he did, I'm indebted to him for my life.'

She put her lips to the strong column of his throat, her hands moving inside his shirt to the damp firmness of his body.

Some time later he moved her away from him and looked into her flushed face, still languidly sensuous from his lovemaking, and took a ragged breath. 'Wow!' he said huskily.

And they smiled wonderingly at each other.

'Seriously, Brooke, do you fancy becoming a station wife?' he asked. 'Will it be too lonely for you after the city?'

Shaking her head emphatically, she hastened to reassure him. 'There must be some magic out at Terebori Downs, because I think I found my gold there, at the rainbow's end. I knew I felt at home somehow, the moment I stepped into the homestead, until you came

over all caveman again.' She touched her fist to his
chin.

'I did rather, didn't I? I wanted you all to myself.
Dave's always been welcome out at the Downs, but on
that particular day I could have thrown him off the
place without the slightest compunction.' Although he
smiled his eyes were steely.

'Caveman or no caveman,' she sighed, 'I'll just have
to marry you.' Her eyes twinkled. 'My brother Craig
would never forgive me if I refused you. When I told
the family I could be transferred into the country Craig
suggested I keep my eyes open for a rich cow cockie so
that he could have a pony of his own.'

'Oh, he did, did he?' Kley's fingers moved over the
smooth skin of her midriff. 'A very sensible boy, your
brother. Remind me to give him a whole string of
horses,' he said huskily, his lips claiming hers in con-
tentment.

A week later Jilly Martin opened a gilded wedding
invitation and she smiled with self-satisfaction. Yes, she
did so like all the ends to be tied.